About the Author

He studied philosophy in undergraduate school and English Literature in graduate school. He has a good sense of humor, though sometimes he has trouble transmitting that into his fiction.

Reflections on a Dream

Paul Devito

Reflections on a Dream

Olympia Publishers
London

www.olympiapublishers.com
OLYMPIA PAPERBACK EDITION

Copyright © Paul Devito 2023

The right of Paul Devito to be identified as author of
this work has been asserted in accordance with sections 77 and 78 of
the Copyright, Designs and Patents Act 1988.

All Rights Reserved

No reproduction, copy or transmission of this publication
may be made without written permission.
No paragraph of this publication may be reproduced,
copied or transmitted save with the written permission of the publisher,
or in accordance with the provisions
of the Copyright Act 1956 (as amended).

Any person who commits any unauthorised act in relation to
this publication may be liable to criminal
prosecution and civil claims for damage.

A CIP catalogue record for this title is
available from the British Library.

ISBN: 978-1-80439-289-8

This is a work of fiction.
Names, characters, places and incidents originate from the writer's
imagination. Any resemblance to actual persons, living or dead, is
purely coincidental.

First Published in 2023

Olympia Publishers
Tallis House
2 Tallis Street
London
EC4Y 0AB

Printed in Great Britain

Dedication

I dedicate this book to my brother Marco.

Acknowledgements

I thank everyone in my family for their support.

Chapter 1

We were sitting by the lake, our feet dangling in the water. The sun was setting over the opposite hill, and the orange glow reflected off the water. The moon was already up, hovering over the horizon. All was at peace. She had picked me up from the airport the day before, and now we were in the Adirondacks on a camping trip, in June. The weather was perfect, not too hot, and the water was warm enough to swim in. We had brought a canoe with us and had spent two hours setting up camp. The pine trees were majestic, and we could drink the water from the lake, it was so clean.

I had been at rehab in California for the last three months. I had been a pot smoker for several years and got very addicted to it. Now I was free from it, and I wanted to start a new life with Jennifer. She had been my girlfriend for several months before I went into rehab and had been instrumental in my seeking recovery. Jennifer was still in college, and I was considerably older. I had taught at her school, and she liked to ask me questions about literature.

I wanted to go for a swim before it got too dark, and before the air got too cool.

"Do you want to swim a little?" I said.

"Yes. Do you want to go naked?" she said.

"Of course," I said.

We took our clothes off, and her tanned skin took on the glow of the setting sun. We slowly slipped into the water and waded out until the water was up to our waists. Then we dove in. We swam out as our arms and legs moved in unison. Stroke by stroke, we plunged ourselves into the water. The sun was disappearing, and we were deep into the lake in a short time. Finally, exhausted, we turned back. After we dried ourselves off, we decided to build a fire. We gathered dry wood and placed each piece carefully in a teepee configuration. We found some logs and placed them to the side until the fire got going. I lit the fire, and she put more twigs on it as it grew. Sparks flew up into the overhanging trees. Her face glowed in the light of the fire. It was beautiful.

"Do you want to have kids one day?" she said.

"Sure. Someday," I said.

"How many?" she said.

"Two is enough, I guess," I said. "What about you?"

"Two or three," she said.

"I don't know about three. Besides, I'm not sure it's a good idea to bring children into this world," I said.

"Why not? We can protect them," she said.

"I think most people have children for selfish reasons, so that somebody will look after them when they get old," I said.

"Why should we be any different?" she said.

I put a log on the fire and watched the sparks fly up into the trees. The fire was getting hot, and it felt good in the cool air.

"A lot of people are not having children these days. They're not even getting married," I said.

"Well, I definitely want to get married," she said.

"Wait a while. You might change your mind," I said.

Suddenly, a log popped, and sparks went flying everywhere. We leaned back, so none of them hit us.

"I'm not going to change my mind about getting married," she said. "I know you've avoided it this long, but I think you're different with me."

"Don't be so sure," I said.

"Now you're being difficult," she said.

"I don't want to argue," I said.

We sat in silence for a long time, staring at the fire. I only wished that she were a few years older. It would have been easier to communicate. She was so beautiful though; she was impossible to resist. Now would be the time I would take out a joint and smoke it. I didn't want to think about pot, but I couldn't help it. I needed to go back to meetings. I didn't think I could stay out in the woods too long. After talking for another half hour, we decided to go to bed. We had separate sleeping bags and were too tired to make love, so we went to sleep. I slept for a few hours, then awakened after a bad dream. I dreamt that I was with friends, smoking pot, smoking crack, and drinking vodka. It was the worst dream of my life. I lay back down but couldn't fall asleep. I kept thinking about my dream. The dream had been worse than the reality. Finally, two or three hours later, I fell asleep.

The birds woke us up early, but I was still tired, so I went back to sleep. Jennifer got up and went to get some water. It was very uncomfortable sleeping on the ground, so I got up and joined her. It was a crisp summer day. The birds were chirping, and the forest was alive. I made a fire with the wood we had collected from the night before. Jennifer sat with me, next to the fire.

"I had a very bad dream last night," I said.

"That's too bad. What was it about?" she said.

"I was with all my old friends, drinking and using," I said. "You were there, too."

"How often does that happen?" she said.

"Frequently enough," I said, "but they say they'll start to go away."

"Do you still have cravings?" she said.

"Yeah. I'd like to be smoking a joint right now," I said.

"Is there anything I can do to help?" she said.

"Just talk me out of it, if I start to do something crazy," I said.

"Let's go for a canoe ride to get your mind off the drugs," she said.

We pushed out the canoe and stepped gingerly inside it. The water was calm as glass, and we could see our reflections in it. We paddled in unison, swirling the water behind each stroke. We moved gracefully together, and the canoe glided quickly through the water. We stopped after a while and drifted slowly on the lake. Then we started up again, slowly, with a steady rhythm. I looked around the lake at the trees and rocks, and I felt grateful that I was clean and sober. She turned around and noticed the calm expression on my face.

"Having fun?" she said.

"Yes. I love being with you out in the woods. The water is so peaceful, isn't it?" I said.

"You handle the canoe well. Where did you learn?" she said.

"I was a summer camp counselor. I ran the waterfront," I said. "Listen, I've been having some terrible cravings for pot. I think we're going to have to cut this trip short. I need to go back to the city and back to my meetings."

"Okay, that's all right with me. I have to do some work for my summer classes," she said.

We turned the canoe around and headed for the campsite. I was feeling pretty anxious and uncomfortable. We broke camp, carefully folding the tent and pulling the stakes out of the ground. After we packed up, we decided to drive to a restaurant and have a big breakfast. Then we drove back to Syracuse and went to her place. Leaving the lake and returning to the city brought on all the old memories of the chaotic life I had lived before. The chaos returned, but in a different form.

Chapter 2

"Why don't we live together?" she said.

"I'll think about it."

"It would be great. You could be there to help me with my homework. We could share the cooking and cleaning chores. It wouldn't be nearly as lonely," she said.

"You're not that lonely, are you?" I said.

"I was when you were away. I have never lived by myself before."

"Don't you enjoy your solitude?"

"You're trying to think of excuses why we shouldn't live together."

"No, I'm not," I said. "I think, for now, it's good the way it is."

"I'm lonely!"

"Honey, I understand that, but I just returned from California. I'm not ready to live with anybody."

"I'm not anybody."

"That's not what I meant," I said.

I was getting frustrated, and all I wanted to do was go home. I was thinking of going over to my old pot dealer's house and getting a small bag, but I thought better of it.

"What do you mean? I just returned from California. Did you have a bad breakup with Laura, and now you don't want to live with me?"

I didn't know how she guessed that, but she was pretty

15

perceptive. I noticed that I was getting in a lot of arguments with Jennifer, and I was getting angry.

"I told you. I was only friends with Laura. We didn't have a bad breakup. Why don't we see how things go over the next few months? Then we'll live together," I said.

"All right, but this is under protest," she said.

"I'm going home now," I said.

"Fine!"

I put my jacket on, made sure I had my cigarettes with me, and left. I lit up as soon as I got in the car, wishing my cigarette was a joint. I thought again about going over to my dealer's house but didn't. I decided to call one of my new friends as soon as I got home. I called my mother first though.

"Hi," she said. "How are you feeling?"

"I feel fine, but Jennifer pisses me off sometimes."

"Did you get in a fight?"

"Sort of. She wants us to live together, and I'm not ready for that."

"You've been through enough for a while, I think," she said.

"I want to teach again, Mom. I've got too much time on my hands."

"That's fine. I'm sure the university will take you back. Are you positive you're ready?"

"I think so," I said.

"Why don't you come over for dinner tomorrow night?"

"Okay. Bye."

I immediately called Gregory. I needed to talk to somebody who understood my feelings.

"Hey, what's up?" he said.

"I had an argument with my girlfriend."

"You've got to apologize to her."

"It wasn't my fault."

"You're still angry. I can hear it in your voice. And even if it wasn't your fault, you should still apologize. You played a part in it. What was it over?"

"She wants to live with me, and I said no."

"Well, you have every right to say that, but it depends on how you say it."

"I thought you were going to take my side."

"There are three sides to every story: your side, her side, and what actually happened."

"You're right, but I don't want to live with her, not yet anyways," I said.

"You have to draw boundaries, but you have to do it in a calm, rational manner," Greg said.

"How can I draw a boundary when she's not rational?"

"Maybe you have to break up with her," he said calmly.

"I don't want to do that! Why do you say that?"

"We suggest that you stay out of a relationship for at least a year."

"Yeah, I did hear that once before. But why?"

"Because the turmoil it will cause in your life will tempt you to go out again."

"You know, after our fight I was tempted to go buy some dope. Maybe you're right."

"It's only a suggestion. Some people have come into the program married for twenty years and manage to keep their marriages alive, but not many."

I thought about what he said and was silent for a second, while I let it sink in. I imagined breaking up with Jennifer, but I was so lonely already. I wanted to do whatever was suggested to stay sober, but I didn't know if I could do this.

"I don't think I want to break up with her, but maybe take some time off," I said.

"That might work. I don't know," he said.

"She's so great though, and I'm in love with her."

"Then stay with her, but you have to avoid getting into fights."

That sounded better to me. I would stay with her and avoid fighting. I felt like I was in turmoil most of the time anyway. I wasn't sure she was the cause.

"I'll talk to you tomorrow, Greg, you've been a big help."

Chapter 3

I slept pretty well considering I had a lot on my mind. I woke up a couple of times during the night and smoked. I used to smoke pot in the middle of the night to put me to sleep, but now I had nothing to rely on. I decided to go to an early morning meeting. I knew Greg would be there.

"Hey, what's up?" I said.

"Good to see you, brother," Greg said.

"This early recovery sucks," I said.

"Tell me about it," he said.

"I think I'll stay with Jennifer, but I'm not going to live with her, and I'm going to try to stay out of arguments."

"Give it a try and see how it works. We do it one day at a time, and we don't drink."

"Yeah, I know. I'm picking up my three-month chip pretty soon," I said.

"Good for you."

Talking to him kept me calm. He was the most serene person I had met so far, and I wanted that serenity.

"Did you talk to her this morning?" he asked.

"No, I figured it would be better to go to a meeting first. I might bring up a topic."

"What would that be?"

"Why is it that I'm always on an emotional rollercoaster?"

"That's a good topic. It's typical of early recovery."

We sat through the meeting, and I got a lot of good feedback on my topic. Afterwards, he introduced me to a couple of guys. I left feeling a lot better and wanted to talk to Jennifer right away. I called her as soon as I got home, but she wasn't there. I left a message and went out to have a late breakfast. I was starting to enjoy being by myself more. I knew it was the right decision to live alone. When I got home, I did some writing and waited impatiently for Jennifer to call. A few hours later she called.

"How are you feeling today?" I said.

"Better. I'm sorry I've been such a bitch. I'm under a lot of pressure at school."

"I know. I've been a pain, too."

"Let's start over, like you got off the plane an hour ago," she said.

"Okay," I said with a laugh.

"Let's make love," she said.

"Not right now, honey. I'm not in the mood. You're a horny girl, aren't you?"

"I guess so, but not more than anyone else, I don't think. I didn't have sex for three months, and now you're criticizing me for being too horny."

"I'm not criticizing you, honey. I'm only pointing out an observation."

"I think you're sexy. We used to have sex all the time."

"I find you sexy, too, but I'm not in the mood right this minute."

"That's all right. Maybe later," she said. "Do you want to come over for a while?"

"I'm going to do some work first. Why don't we plan on having dinner?"

"Okay."

After I hung up, I thought that she was simply difficult to get along with. I sat down to do some writing but couldn't concentrate. Greg's words haunted me. Maybe I did have to break up with Jennifer. All I wanted to do was smoke some pot. I thought about calling Greg but didn't want to bother him. I decided to take a quick nap and paint something when I got up. When I awakened, I wasn't in the mood to paint. I called Jennifer for a lack of anything else to do.

"Hey," I said.

"Hi. What's up?"

"I can't concentrate on my work."

"Why don't you come over? You can help me with mine."

"All right," I said.

I drove over to Jennifer's place but felt out of sorts. I didn't realize how long it would take to feel normal without pot. I was even afraid to drive sober. She welcomed me with a big kiss, and I felt better.

"Do you feel like helping me with my work, or do you want to watch TV?" she said.

"I'll help you."

"Read this article and tell me what you think. It's only about two pages long," she said.

I read the article and couldn't make heads or tails out of it.

"I'm sorry, honey, but I don't understand it either."

"These philosophers are impossible. Who are they trying to impress?" she said.

"Let's kiss a little," I said.

"Do you want to make love?" she said.

"No, just kiss a little."

"Maybe I can put you in the mood."

We kissed for a while and, sure enough, I got a hard-on. We ended up making love, of course, and it helped me to relax. I had forgotten that I was supposed to eat dinner with my mother, so I called her and cancelled.

"Let's go out to dinner. I've got a little money," I said.

"I'd like to try that new Amore restaurant," she said.

"Where is it?"

"In Fayetteville."

"Okay, let's go."

We drove out of town to a little suburban village, where this quaint Italian restaurant was. It wasn't very crowded, as it was early, and we sat by a window. A guy named Matt waited on us, and we enjoyed talking to him on and off throughout the meal. The food was delicious, and we decided to return sometime. We were both in a good mood, and even though we were quiet on the way to her house, the ride was pleasant.

"Do you want to come in? I've got a bottle of wine," she said. "Oh, I'm sorry. I forgot you can't drink either. My fault. Forget I said anything."

"It's all right, honey. It's no big deal. You'll get used to it," I said.

"I should quit drinking, too."

"You don't have a problem with it. Why should you quit?"

"I want to help you," she said.

"Don't be ridiculous. I don't care if you drink."

"I don't need it, and it would be something we could do together, and maybe you could quit smoking."

"I want to quit smoking, but I'm not ready yet."

"I'm still going to quit drinking."

"Suit yourself."

"Come on in anyway," she said.

We went inside, and she immediately walked into the kitchen and poured out the rest of her red wine. I thought the gesture was sweet, and it seemed genuine. I had never had a serious problem with drinking, and it was hardly tempting at all. She never smoked pot, which was great, and I hoped it stayed that way.

"I have some soda. Would you like some?" she said.

"Sure."

"I'm exhausted. That heavy food is putting me to sleep," she said.

"Do you want to go to bed?" I said.

"What did you have in mind?"

"Nothing. I'm talking about sleep."

"We used to have sex three times a day," she said with a pout.

"Isn't once a day enough?"

"I thought you liked it."

"Of course I like it, but not all the time. You're young. You wouldn't understand."

"I hate when you say that. I can understand everything."

"You don't lack brains, only experience," I said softly.

"Well, let's take a nap and see how we feel later," she said.

"Good idea."

We lay on the couch, holding each other, and fell asleep. Half an hour later, I awakened. I was used to taking short naps. She wanted to sleep some more, so I turned on the television and listened to a jazz show. After a while, I got bored, left her on the couch, and went home. I called Gregory the minute I got into my apartment.

"What's up?" he said.

"I have this terrible urge to smoke pot," I said.

"You've got to take your mind off of it. There's a late-night meeting if you want to go, or you can stay on the phone with me until the urge passes."

"I'm not going out again tonight," I said. "I'll talk to you.

What have you been up to today?'"

"I went over to my girlfriend's house. We hung out and cooked ribs."

"I love ribs. Where's the best place to get ribs in this town?" I asked.

"Dinosaur Barbecue, I think, but there are a few places, like Birdland, Kirby's."

"Did you watch the basketball game today?"

"Some of it, but we had the kids with us, so we couldn't watch too much."

"How long are these urges going to last? I think about smoking all the time," I said.

"It depends. I didn't smoke pot, so it may be different, but in a few months, most of the urges should go away," he said. "In the meantime, go to a lot of meetings. That'll help."

I was getting more relaxed talking to him. The strong urge had mostly passed, but I stayed on the phone with him for quite a while longer.

"I'm still having problems with my girlfriend," I said.

"I'm not surprised. Those kinds of things don't just go away," he said.

"What am I supposed to do?" I said, exasperated.

"Maybe you should ask for a little space. That way you can still be with her while getting a break."

"I think I will. She won't be too happy about it, but I need some solitude. I don't care how lonely it gets."

I thought about her reaction and knew she would lose her temper. I hoped she would understand and realize that I really didn't want to break up with her. I would have to be very careful about how I said it.

"Listen. I'm going to call her right now. I'll talk to you later,"

I said.

I waited a few minutes and thought about what I would say. Nothing sounded right. It would be harsh, no matter how I put it. I dialed slowly and kept thinking.

"Hi. Still sleeping?" I said.

"No. I'm up. I was going to call you."

"Listen, sweetheart, I was talking to a friend of mine, and he agrees that I should concentrate on my recovery and not see you as much."

"What does concentrating on your recovery have to do with seeing me?" she said.

"Well, we get in a lot of arguments, and they make me want to smoke pot."

"That sounds like a lousy excuse to me," she said, and hung up.

I didn't know what to do at first. I thought about calling her back, but then I figured it might be better to leave her alone. I knew my excuse had sounded weak, but it was true. I was going to call Gregory again but decided I would see him in the morning. I called Murray instead.

"Hey, what's up?" he said.

"I told my girlfriend that I needed some space, and she hung up on me."

He laughed, and then calmed down.

"What did you expect?"

"Actually, that's pretty much what I expected. I thought she might yell at me, but apparently hanging up has a greater effect and uses less energy," I said, laughing.

"Well, at least you can laugh about it," he said.

"I probably won't think it's too funny tomorrow. I still love her, but we get into so many arguments. I need a break."

"Then you did the right thing."

"But what if she goes out with somebody else?"

"I guess that's the risk you have to take, but if I know women, she'll like the challenge of getting you back even more."

"You think so?" I said.

"Sure. Listen. Don't worry about it now. Things will look better in the morning. Get some sleep, and I'll talk to you tomorrow."

After I hung up, I felt very agitated. I wanted to call Jennifer and patch things up but was worried she would scream at me or hang up on me again. I went to bed but couldn't sleep. I was having the worst thoughts. I hated everybody and everything. After tossing and turning for a few hours, I decided to call Jennifer in the middle of the night.

"Hello?"

"Hi, sweetheart."

"Why are you calling me at two in the morning?"

"I want to apologize," I said.

"Apology accepted. Now let me get some sleep. I have classes early in the morning."

"Okay," I said, and hung up.

I thought I would feel better, but I didn't. I had a miserable, restless night and woke up in a terrible mood.

Chapter 4

I could never sleep in, so I got up at seven and took a shower. I had some coffee and felt better being awake. All I could think about was Jennifer and her being angry with me. I called my mother, which I regularly did early in the morning.

"Hi," I said.

"How are you doing today, honey?" she said.

"Not very well. Last night I told Jennifer I needed some space but changed my mind and called her in the middle of the night. She's pretty angry with me."

"Did you apologize?"

"Sort of."

"It'll work itself out. Give her a little time and call her tomorrow."

"Thanks, Mom."

"Bye."

"Bye," I said, feeling better.

I went to my early morning meeting and saw Greg. He was standing outside talking to a girl named Julie, smoking a cigarette. Julie was very pretty, about five feet two and blonde. She had a great laugh, which attracted me immediately. She also had a nice ass.

"How are you doing today?" Greg said.

"Not very well. I told Jennifer I needed some space, and she hung up on me."

"Oh no, not more relationship problems," Julie said.

"Sounds like you're familiar with them," I said.

"I've seen everything. I just got out of a relationship with a man who beat me," she said.

"Well, at least you got out," I said.

"It only took me five years," she said, and laughed.

"It's good you're laughing about it," I said.

"I wasn't laughing for a long time."

"I'm sorry to hear that," I said.

"It's my own fault for sticking around, but you can't see any escape route until somebody helps you," she said.

"Like alcoholism," Greg said.

"Sometimes they go together, as in my case," Julie said. "You didn't hit your girlfriend, did you?"

"No, no, nothing like that. I'm not a violent person. We argue a lot."

"Well, verbal violence is just as bad," she said.

I thought about what she said and wondered if I were really abusive toward Jennifer. I never called her names or put her down. I had too much respect for her.

"I don't put her down," I said. "We only argue about trivial stuff, like sex."

"Sex isn't trivial," Julie said.

"No, I guess not. Our sexual life is pretty good, but she's young. She wants to do it all the time."

"I never heard a man complain about that!" She laughed.

"I could use that problem," Greg said.

"We have interesting intellectual conversations though, too, so it's not all bad, and I guess we really love each other," I said.

"Did you meet in recovery?" Julie asked.

"No. I met her when I was still smoking pot, and then I went to rehab for three months. I've only been back a few days."

28

"I'm sure you'll work things out. Is she an alcoholic?" Julie said.

"No. She's normal, which is great. I don't have to deal with that. She wants to quit drinking for me, even though she doesn't have a problem, but I think she expects me to quit smoking, which I'm not really prepared to do."

"Sounds like a great girl," Julie said.

"She is. No doubt about it, which is why I want to work things out."

I thought about how great Jennifer was and what a fool I was for asking for more space. I would call her today, I thought. I wasn't going to wait until tomorrow. The meeting started, and we all went inside. The topic was resentments, and I honestly couldn't think of anyone that I really resented. I considered myself fortunate, but I thought I had probably created some resentments in others along the way. I had isolated myself so much, that I hadn't really hurt anybody, or so I thought. I had worried my mother to death, but that was all I could think of.

Then I thought about Laura. She probably resented the hell out of me. I left her high and dry in California with no way to reach me. I had left the others, too. They probably weren't too happy about it either. After the meeting, Julie, Greg, and I met outside for a smoke.

"What do you do for a living, Paul?" Julie asked.

"Nothing right now. I used to teach English at the university. Now I'm writing and painting."

"A man with talent. I like that," she said, winking at me.

"What about you, Julie?" I said.

"I wait on tables at a restaurant in Fayetteville."

"Amore?"

"No. Kirby's"

"I've eaten there before. The food is good."

"Come in and see me sometime. Bring your girlfriend."

"I don't know. She might get jealous," I said with a laugh, playing it off.

"Don't bring her then." She laughed.

I hadn't flirted with another woman in a long time, and it felt good. Julie was quite a bit older than Jennifer, which I liked, but of course she had little education. I wasn't a snob about it, but I wondered what we'd have to talk about after a while.

"Bring Greg instead," she said, giving Greg a hug.

"I will," I said.

"I have to go," Julie said.

"Nice piece of ass, isn't she?" Greg said.

"Too bad we both have girlfriends," I said.

"That never stopped a man," Greg said.

"I don't know what to do about Jennifer," I said.

"Take it easy with her. That's all. Don't spend so much time with her," he said.

"I have to take off, too. I'll call you later," I said, thinking that I had to telephone Jennifer right away.

When I went home, I paced the floor for about half an hour, thinking of what I would say to her. I called her and found that she was still at class. I was going to leave a message but changed my mind. I took a badly needed nap and woke up two hours later. I called her again.

"Hey, how are you?" I said.

"Well, I couldn't get back to sleep last night, so I was a zombie in class."

"I'm sorry. It's my fault."

"I know it's your fault," she said, calmly.

"I apologize again. I was a fool to ask for more space. I love you to death."

"I forgive you again. Now can we get back to normal?"

"Absolutely," I said excitedly.

"Why don't you come over?"

"All right."

I took a very hot shower, which felt good after my nap, and I put on some clothes. When I arrived at her place, she had all the curtains drawn, and candles lit everywhere. The apartment looked like a small brothel. I got the hint right away.

"Are you trying to seduce me?" I said. "Because you don't have to go to all this trouble."

"You mean we can have sex?" she said, surprised.

"Why are you so surprised? I can do it once a year," I said, winking at her. "My friends find it very strange that I don't want to have sex all the time."

"I find it strange too," she said.

"You'll feel differently when you get older," I said.

"Oh, here we go again with the older stuff. Do you want me to date somebody my own age?"

"Of course not, but you're not going to want to fuck like a bunny when you're in your middle thirties."

"I'll be in my prime then, of course. I'll want to do it often. You're not in your prime. I understand that, but you used to do it with me all the time. I think you don't like my body any more," she said.

"I like your body, but the excitement of the first few months wears off," I said, thinking about how much I loved to fuck Laura.

"The excitement hasn't worn off for me. You sound like we've been married for ten years."

"Can we please stop arguing about sex all the time?" I said.

"If we do it now, I'll stop arguing," she said laughing.

"I can't stay mad at you," I said.

"I kissed her, and she slipped her hand down my pants. I got hard and put my hands on her ass. The next thing you know, we were rolling around, tearing each other's clothes off and fucking our brains out, but I noticed she didn't come. I was beginning to get paranoid about making women come, but I didn't want to bring it up and start another argument.

"That felt good," I said.

"I liked it, too," she said. "Are you hungry?"

"Yes."

We took a shower and ate some lunch. She had studying to do, so I went home and did some writing.

Chapter 5

After writing for a while, I got bored and watched a movie on TV. I was thinking about Julie, who I knew was working that night, and I decided to go into the restaurant. Jennifer kept pretty close tabs on me, but I would tell her that I went over to my mother's. It was still early in the afternoon, so I figured Julie would have time to talk to me. When I got to the restaurant, Julie was just pulling up.

"Hey, what's up, kid?" I said.

"You're here kind of early, aren't you?" she said.

"I thought you might have more time to talk."

"Grab a table. I'll be out in a few minutes," she said.

I could tell she was glad to see me, even though she didn't know me at all. She had her hair pulled back in a ponytail, and strands of hair along the side of her face. She looked cute as hell. She came to my table a few minutes later.

"What are you doing here?" she said.

"You invited me, so I thought I'd take you up on it."

"I'm glad you showed up. I rarely have any friends come in here. I had to give up all my old friends, as I'm sure you did. I get pretty lonely at times," she said.

"We'll have to do something about that," I said, winking at her.

"I thought you had a girlfriend."

"I guess so, but we're not getting along very well."

"Oh yeah, you fight about sex all the time," she said,

laughing.

"She's too young for me," I said.

"I've never heard of a woman being too young for a man," she said.

"I like mature women, somewhere between ninety and a hundred years old," I said, laughing.

"I'm too young for you then. That's too bad."

"You're just right for me," I said.

"Are you saying I look ninety years old?"

"Closer to one hundred," I said.

"I'll be right back," she said.

I watched her go about her duties. Her ass wiggled in the nicest way. I could tell she was somewhat disorganized. It took her a long time to do something on the computer. She took an order from one table and brought me a soda. She was very friendly with the customers. Everybody seemed to like her. She couldn't stop and chat, so I told her I would see her later at a meeting. I left her a big tip and took off. When I got home, there were three messages from Jennifer. She always got pissed off when she didn't know where I was. I called her.

"Hi," I said.

"Where have you been? I've been calling you all afternoon."

"I went over to my mother's for a little while," I said.

"Oh, how is she?"

"She's fine. What's up?"

"I don't know. I need help with my work. Do you feel like coming over?"

"Sure, and let's go out for dinner," I said.

When I arrived, she came to the door in her nightie.

"I thought you needed help with your work," I said.

"I do. I'm dressed comfortably is all. You don't mind, do

you?"

"I don't care, but you've got to be serious about your work or you'll never get into graduate school."

"I'm doing fine. Don't worry about it."

I walked in, and all the candles were lit again. I was getting angry and was thinking of leaving, but I cooled off. There was absolutely no reason for me to be upset, but I still felt that she wasn't serious about her work.

"When I was in school, I didn't even have a steady girlfriend. All I did was study," I said.

"I study all the time," she said.

"I know you do. I don't know why I'm upset, honey. Let's see what you're reading now."

"Sit down, dear, relax," she said.

She turned on the lights in her living room and blew out some of the candles. Then she walked into her bedroom and put on a robe. I should have fucked her right then and got on with the studying afterwards, but I wasn't in the mood.

"What does phallogocentric mean?" she asked.

"It means a male-centered or oriented text that is also logocentric. Chauvinistic would be a simpler way to put it."

"Oh, I see. Well, why couldn't he say it that way?"

"Who knows, honey," I said.

"I have an idea, Paul. Let's get married," she said.

"Oh, don't bring that up now. We haven't gone out long enough."

"We've gone out enough. We love each other, don't we? Why do we have to wait if we know it's all right?" she said.

"I thought we settled this when I said I didn't want to live together."

"This would be different. It would be a lifetime commitment,

35

and we could plan on having children and teaching together. It would be great."

"When did you come up with this scheme?" I said.

"Yesterday!"

"Well, it's not a good idea," I said, trying to contain my anger.

I almost walked right out the door, but I didn't want to hurt her feelings any more. I appreciated the fact that she was infatuated with me, but I wasn't anywhere near ready to get married. She started to cry, so I put my arms around her and held her tight.

"We'll get married someday, honey, just not right now," I said. "My life is in turmoil. I can't do the simplest things. You're going to have to be patient."

"How long do I have to wait?"

"I don't know. At least a year or two," I said, thinking about Laura.

"Who knows how I'll feel by then," she said.

"If you can't feel strongly for a year or two, how are you going to make a life-long commitment?" I said angrily.

"All right, all right, don't get upset."

"I'm going home," I said.

"No, don't leave, not while you're angry," she said.

I got up and left in a huff. As I was walking out the door, I told her I would call her the next day. I decided to go back out to the restaurant where Julie worked. It was later in the evening, but they were still serving.

"Hi," she said.

"I missed you," I said with a laugh.

"I thought I'd see you at the meeting later," she said.

"I got into another argument with my girlfriend, so I'm

dining alone," I said.

"Great."

I sat down and looked at the menu, while Julie got me a cup of coffee. I ordered the ribs and hoped she would have a little time to talk to me. When she brought the food, she sat down for a couple of minutes.

"What part of town are you living in?" I said.

"The Westcott area," she said.

"That's a coincidence. So am I."

"There are a lot of drugs in that area now," she said.

"It's happening all over town. I'm going to move out here, I think," I said.

"So am I, as soon as I can afford it."

"What was your drug of choice?" I asked.

"Drinking mostly, but I smoked crack sometimes, too," she said.

I nodded, and she left the table to do her work. I thought about the times I did cocaine and smoked crack, which weren't many, and had horrible memories. I thought hard at that moment if I wanted to get involved with an alcoholic, since I had already been through it with Laura. Julie came back to the table a few minutes later.

"Paul," she said slowly, "I don't know if I can handle another boyfriend at this time. I need you as a sober friend."

"I was thinking the same thing," I said.

"I'm glad, because all these guys keep hitting on me, and I know they only want one thing," she said.

"I know, honey. I won't do that to you."

She left the table with a small smile on her face. I paid the bill, leaving her a big tip again, and left. I decided to go to the late meeting and realized that my anger toward Jennifer had already disappeared. At the meeting, I saw Gregory outside, having a cigarette.

"Hey, what's up?" I said.

"Nothing much," he said.

"I saw Julie a few minutes ago at the restaurant," I said.

"Trying to get some of that ass, I see," he said.

"No, we're only friends," I said.

"Sure, whatever."

"Well, for now anyways," I said.

"What about Jennifer?" he said.

"I got mad at her earlier, but now I'm cool."

The meeting started, and we went inside. I was surprised at how many people were there. I hardly knew anybody, and I felt slightly ill at ease. The topics were fear and anger, and I could identify with almost everything that was said. Afterwards, Gregory and I stood out in the cool evening and smoked.

"Are you going to call Jennifer tonight?" he said.

"Probably not," I said. "I don't want her to wear the pants in the family, even though I think she already does."

"Sounds that way to me." He laughed.

"Actually, I think neither of us is in control of the situation," I said.

"You can get some sort of control by lying back," he said.

"What do you mean?" I said.

"Don't see her so often. Don't call so much. Just lay back," he said.

"I'll try that," I said. "I'll see you later."

"Bye."

I wasn't going to call Jennifer that night, but I couldn't resist. I thought about what Greg had said to me, but I still wanted to call her. She was still studying when I called.

"Hi," she said. "Are you still mad at me?"

"No."

"Do you want to spend the night?" she said.

"No."

"You're still mad. I can tell."

"Only irritated."

"I'm sorry," she said.

"I'm sorry, too."

"We don't have to get married or live together. Everything is fine the way it is," she said.

"I'm glad you feel that way," I said.

I was feeling better now and thought that I might spend the night with her, but I decided against it. I would try to "lay back" as Greg put it.

"We should spend a little less time together. It would be better for us," I said.

"You're not breaking up with me, are you?"

"No, of course not, but I can't take all this drama," I said.

"Okay. You call me whenever you want. I won't bother you," she said.

After I hung up, I felt better. I was going to try to gain a little more control. I went to bed, feeling good, but had too much coffee in me to go to sleep. I was in a half sleep later in the night and had an intense dream. I only remember bits and pieces of the dream. I don't believe you can know the unconscious. It was like a surrealistic fiction that began with me fucking Jennifer. She was on top and was wearing a bizarre mask. It was more like her face was painted in a very strange way. She was talking to me while we were fucking, but words wouldn't come out of my mouth to respond. She slapped me, and then cut my dick off. I was in tremendous pain, but I couldn't scream. The next thing you know,

Jennifer turned into Laura, and the colors on her face changed. Then Laura turned into Julie, who had no mask. I woke up with a huge hard on and masturbated right away. I laughed to myself and went back to sleep.

When I awakened, it was getting late, and I wanted to do some writing before I went out. I called Jennifer, but she was already gone. I felt a growing distance between us, and it bothered me. I called Greg and he was home.

"Hey, what's up?" he said.

"Nothing. I was thinking that my relationship with Jennifer isn't going very well."

"I told you what to do."

"Yeah, and I'm going to try it. I talked to her last night and told her that I needed to cool off a little," I said.

"So, what's the problem?"

"I feel like we're getting a divorce or something."

"Look, it's not unusual to feel very needy in early recovery. You have to rely more on us."

"That's pretty much what I did in California, but I still had a relationship."

"Can't you spend more time alone when you're not at meetings?" he said.

"I don't know. I get really lonely if I'm not with someone or on the phone."

"You'll get stronger as time goes by."

"Thanks for reassuring me. I'll see you at the meeting," I said.

Suddenly, I had a tremendous urge to smoke pot, and I didn't know what to do. I obsessed on this urge for about an hour, then called my pot dealer. I knew his number by heart. He was home, and I told him I would be over in ten minutes. After I hung up, I changed my mind. Then I changed my mind again and went over to his home. He was glad to see me, but I felt like a criminal, which I was, and left quickly. I went to the store and bought some rolling papers. When I got home, there was a message from Jennifer to call her. I wanted to talk to her, but I was on a mission. I rolled a joint and smoked it. The pot was good, and I was high as hell. I put my head back on the couch and closed my eyes. Now what was I going to do? I called Jennifer.

"Hi," I said.

"Where have you been?" she asked.

"I have a confession to make. I got high a few minutes ago."

"You're high? But you were doing so well. What triggered it?"

"I don't know, but I feel guilty."

"Sometimes those things happen, but don't get back in the habit of doing it all the time."

"No, this is the last time. It feels really weird. I obsessed over it for a while. The impulse was so powerful. I don't know what to do," I said.

"Why don't you sleep it off?"

"I don't think I can sleep right now. Maybe I'll go to a meeting."

"Don't go anywhere. I'll be right over."

After I hung up, I put some jazz on. I loved listening to Miles Davis. It wasn't long before she arrived.

"How do you feel now?" she said, as she walked in the door.

"Better now. I've adjusted."

"Don't let it feel too good."

"No, I am not going to do it again. This day is wasted, and I like being straight. I'm such an idiot," I said.

"Don't put yourself down. You have an addiction. I'm sure

plenty of people don't get perfectly sober the first time."

"You're being very understanding," I said.

"Well, I love you. I like it when you're vulnerable and not in control all the time."

"I guess I'm different when I'm sober, aren't I?" I said.

"I'm not used to the new you, that's all. When you're high, you're mellow, and nothing bothers you."

"I know. I'm not used to the new me either, but I like being clearheaded and able to write."

I looked at her more closely and noticed she was wearing a low-cut shirt. I got horny by looking at her fleshy tits. She noticed me looking and widened her eyes.

"Want some?" she said.

"Yeah."

She stood up and slowly undressed in front of me, leaving her panties on. I got hard and let her take my pants off, putting my cock in her mouth. When I was stoned I could keep it hard for a long time, but it was difficult for me to come. She slowly licked my cock and balls, sliding up and down, tantalizing me. I reached down and slipped my hand under her panties, which were already wet. I rubbed her clit, slowly, in circles until it was hard. Then I kissed her breasts and stomach, moving down slowly to her pussy, while she continued to suck my cock. After I licked her clit, with two fingers inside her, rubbing her g-spot, she came very slowly and for a long time, giving out deep moans. While she was coming, I put my very hard cock inside her, pumping very slowly at first. Then I increased the speed of my thrusts and their depth. She kept saying, "Keep going, keep going." Finally, I came.

"Ahhh," I said.

"How was that?" she said.

"Fantastic," I said.

"Are you tired now?" she said.

"Yeah?"

"Why don't you go to sleep, and we'll get together tomorrow."

I slept all afternoon and woke up later that evening. I had the most powerful cravings to smoke more pot, but I flushed the rest of it. Then I tried to sleep again, but I couldn't. I tossed and turned for several hours, so I decided to go to a late-night meeting. I announced that I had "gone back out" and they concentrated their attentions on me. Some were outright cruel, but most were very sympathetic. I had a very rough night that night, with all kinds of terrible thoughts, but I got through it. In the morning, I made coffee and had a few cigarettes. Then I called Jennifer.

"Hey," I said.

"Hey, yourself. How do you feel?"

"Pretty shitty, actually."

"Did you get any sleep?" she said.

"Not really."

"I have to go to class in a little while. Do you want to have lunch?"

"Sure, call me later."

I dragged my ass into the shower and stood under the hot water for several minutes. I was so angry at myself for smoking the night before. Now I would have to fight the cravings all over again and start counting the days. I went to the meeting, and Greg welcomed me with open arms.

"I heard. Don't worry about it. At least you're back. It could be worse. You could still be out there."

"I'm so angry," I said.

"I know, I know. I've been there. Pick yourself up, dust

yourself off, and start over."

"I'm trying. It's not easy. All I want to do is smoke pot. But then I don't want to, either. I don't know what I want," I said.

"Come on now. You don't want to be high all the time. You've got to give this a chance."

"I know, but the cravings are so strong."

"That's the price you have to pay," he said. "At least you know you've done it before."

We went into the meeting, and a lot of people shook my hand, which made me feel better. I didn't hear anything that was said. My mind kept telling me that I had to stay. After the meeting, Greg and I and Murray stood outside and smoked.

"Do you feel better?" Murray said.

"A little," I said.

"You would be wise to go to three meetings a day for a while," Greg said.

"Yeah, I was thinking the same thing," I said.

Julie came outside a little later and hung out with us. She was wearing a simple dress and had her blonde hair pulled back. She looked great.

"How are you doing?" she asked me.

"Not very well, thank you," I said.

"Shake it off. Today is another day."

I was feeling miserable, and nothing anybody said to me was going to make me feel better. I wanted to go home and smoke some pot, but I didn't. I went home and called Jennifer.

"Hi, sweetheart," I said.

"How are you doing?" she said.

"Not very well. I have terrible cravings and mental obsessions. It's really bad."

"I'm sorry to hear that. Want me to come over?"

"Would you?" I said.

"Sure."

She took her time coming over. It seemed like hours before she arrived. She was wearing a classic grey skirt, above the knees, and a white blouse. She looked hot, but I didn't want to fuck her.

"Do you want to make love?" she said.

"Not really," I said. "I don't feel good."

"I brought some homework with me. Do you want to help me?"

"I can't right now. I want to listen to music and talk, talk about nothing."

"Fine with me," she said.

We turned on the stereo and talked for an hour, until we fell asleep in each other's arms. It felt good to be close to her in my time of need. When we awakened, it was time for lunch.

"Are you hungry?" she asked.

"Not really."

"Why don't I make us a salad?"

"Okay."

"Do you blame me for smoking last night?"

"Well, I think if we hadn't argued ever since I came back to Syracuse, I wouldn't have needed to," I said.

"I knew you blamed me," she said angrily.

"Relax, honey, I think the arguing was mostly my fault, and I don't want to get in an argument right now. I love you, and I need you. I don't want to fight," I said.

"I shouldn't be going out with a drug addict anyway. I'm sure I could do much better," she said.

"Ow, that hurt. Why are you trying to hurt me?"

"I'm sorry. I didn't mean it. I'm upset is all."

"You lose your temper so easily. Why is that?" I said.

"I take after my father."

She made a salad as we talked, and I was getting hungry watching her.

"What did your father yell about?" I said.

"What didn't he yell about! I had a boyfriend in high school, and he was never good enough for my dad. My father thought I shouldn't even have a boyfriend at that age. He was very strict," she said.

"When am I going to meet your father?" I said.

"I don't know, soon. They're coming up for parents' weekend. I told them a lot about you, and they're impressed," she said.

"Well, I'm sure you didn't tell them that I was a big pot smoker."

"No, of course not."

"What did you tell them?"

"That you're a nice guy with a lot of talent."

"Thanks. I guess that'll do."

We ate the salad, but I was going crazy with my cravings. I wished that I hadn't touched anything. I had been doing fine. After lunch, we studied together, and that took my mind off the pot. I was thinking to myself while she read out loud. I was wondering what we could know if language were in motion and pure repetition was impossible. We could know that God doesn't exist; that was decidable enough, and it would never change. But what about multiple voices as Derrida kept pointing out? I thought maybe he was missing the point, because there are infinite voices since there are infinite interpretations to every text. I kept thinking about it and remembered my travels into philosophy while stoned. My brain got tired, and I went back to my cravings.

"That's enough studying for now," she said. "I can't concentrate any more. These philosophers are crazy."

"They're not crazy, only obsessive-compulsive."

"They get one idea in their heads and go to any lengths to prove it. What's the point?" she said.

"Some of their ideas are pretty good, but they're fucked up as people," I said. "My father said he'd like to see Kierkegaard go out and play a round of golf." I laughed.

"You're a bit of a philosopher, too," she said. "Be careful what you say." She laughed.

"A little bit is all right. It's when you make it your life's work that you have to watch out," I said. "These guys have no sense of humor."

"Do you want to go out and do something?" she said.

"Like what?"

"I don't know. We could go to a movie or go to the museum," she said.

"Why don't we rent a movie and stay in," I said.

"Okay with me. What do you want to see?"

"Why don't you go and pick one out, maybe a Fellini or something."

"I'll find something good, a French movie or one of those slow Chinese films."

She took off, and I watched the television while listening to jazz. I put on some light porn on TV. and massaged myself a little as I watched. When Jennifer returned, I attacked her. I fucked her so hard I ran out of breath and had to rest. We put on this French film, which I didn't like very much. Later, I told her I had to go to a meeting, and she said she would call me around dinnertime.

When I got to the meeting, Gregory was there, and I was

very grateful that he was. We had a smoke outside, and I was hoping Julie would show up, but she didn't. I brought up the topic at the meeting, and it was about cravings, and the mental obsession to drink or use. I got some good feedback and felt much better afterwards. Outside again, Gregory and I talked. I told him I had thrown out the rest of the pot, and he told me to stay close to the meetings. I went home, and the cravings started again. I called Jennifer, but she wasn't home. Now I was left to myself to think all the terrible thoughts that come with early recovery. I took a hot bath and closed my eyes. All I could see in my imagination was smoking a joint. I got out quietly and called Jennifer again. This time she was home.

"Hey," I said.

"How do you feel?" she said.

"Shitty."

"Do you want me to come over?"

"Would you?"

"Sure."

She came right over, and I was so glad to see her.

"Tell me what you're going through," she said.

"I have these awful physical cravings, and I keep thinking about getting high."

"How can I help you?"

"Talking about it seems to help, but I have to also talk about it with people who have gone through the same thing," I said.

"I really don't know what to say. Maybe you should hang out at the hall all day for a while."

"I was thinking the same thing, and that's what Gregory suggested, too."

"Do you want a nice backrub?"

"That would be great."

She rubbed my back and my ass, and it felt great. I turned over, and she gave me a hand job. Every time I closed my eyes, I kept thinking about smoking pot. It was driving me crazy.

"Let's get out of Syracuse after the semester is over," I said.

"That would be great. Where do you want to go?"

"I don't know, maybe Italy or something."

"Wouldn't that be wonderful? Can we afford it, Paul?"

"I think so. I'll discuss it with my mother. This town drives me crazy. I'm so bored here."

"You lived in Florence, right?"

"And Rome when I was a kid."

"Okay, let's do it. I can waitress over there, or even teach English. Maybe I can even finish my studies there."

"Without the pot, I can concentrate on finishing this novel, and that'll help me stay clean for a year or two."

"Show me your pictures of Italy again. I'm getting excited now," she said.

I went into my room and dug up my old pictures of Italy. We sifted through them, and I reminisced about my year in Florence. I had written about my experiences there, and mostly about the women I had known there.

"How much would a small one-bedroom apartment cost now?" she asked.

"I don't know. We might be able to find one on the outskirts for twelve hundred dollars, or something like that. When I lived there, I paid four hundred dollars for a place right in the city."

"Call your mom."

"Okay."

I called my mother and told her I had smoked pot again the night before.

"Oh, honey, but why?"

"I don't know, Mom. I haven't felt comfortable since I've come back to Syracuse. I was doing better in California, but what I'd really like to do is go to Italy," I said.

"Italy?"

"Don't you think that's a good idea? I'd be away from everything, and Jennifer wants to come, too."

"That would be pretty expensive," she said.

"We can afford it, Mom. It would only be for a year or two."

"A year or two? I was thinking maybe for a month or two," she said.

"I've got to get out of this town, Ma. Please let me go. It'll be good for me."

"I'll think about it," she said.

"Thanks, bye." I said to Jennifer, "She'll think about it, which means probably yes,"

"Oh, I'm so happy," she said.

I got excited thinking about Florence. Jennifer would be done in another two weeks, so it was time to start planning. I called my cousin in Rome and talked to her for a while about prices of apartments. She told me she could go to Florence and get me a place for a thousand dollars, not too far from the center of town. I had almost forgotten about my cravings when they came back with a vengeance.

"I don't know what to do about these cravings," I said.

"Maybe you could go to detox for a couple of days, and they can give you some medication," she said.

"No, I'm not doing that. I have to go to another meeting right now," I said.

"Okay, I'll see you later," she said.

I went to the hall, but the next meeting wasn't starting for another half hour. Greg wasn't there, so I talked to this golfer

50

whom I had met, named Larry.

"I don't know what to do with myself. I'm so uncomfortable," I said.

"Hang out here all day. It's not safe out there," he said. "I have twelve years, and I still spend a lot of time here."

"I do feel a lot better when I'm here," I said.

"After a while you can return to doing one meeting a day, but for now try three," he said.

I lit a cigarette and looked out over the parking lot. No one was there, except Larry and I, and he was making me feel so much better.

"Can I go golfing with you guys sometime?" I said.

"Sure, anytime."

"What kind of work do you do?" I asked.

"I used to be a stockbroker, but now I'm retired."

"Can I use your phone for a second?"

"Sure."

I called Gregory and talked him into coming to the hall. I talked to Larry for a while until Gregory and some of the others started showing up. I was pleasantly surprised to see Julie.

"Hey, what's up, kiddo?" I said to Julie.

"Nothing. How are you feeling?" she said.

"A little better. I still have bad cravings. I'm thinking about going to Italy for a while to get away from everything," I said.

"Italy sounds nice. Are you taking your girlfriend?"

"Yeah, but I'm having second thoughts about that part."

"Do you have family or friends in Italy?"

"Yeah, I have some cousins and a couple of friends in Florence," I said.

Greg walked up, after getting a cup of coffee inside, and lit a cigarette.

"What's in Florence?" he said.

"I'm thinking of going there for a while to get away from everything."

"I wish I could go to Italy," he said.

"I'd like to go, too," Julie said, blinking her eyes.

"Maybe I'll take you," I said to Julie.

"Your girlfriend won't like that," she said.

"By the time he gets to Italy, she won't be able to say anything." Greg laughed.

After a while the meeting started, and I felt uncomfortable the whole way through, but I was glad I was there. The topic was the obsession of drinking, and I could identify with everything that was said. When the meeting ended, I had the sudden urge to go smoke pot. I told Greg about it outside, and he started to lecture me.

"I don't need a lecture," I said. "You've never lectured me before. Why would you start now?"

"I'm sorry. I know lectures don't work, but you have to get a grip, or you'll have to go back to rehab," he said.

"You'll be all right," Julie said. "Do you want to hang out with me and talk?"

"I'd like that," I said.

Julie and I went to her place. It was nicely decorated in green and blue, and it had a great atmosphere about it.

"Next time you can come to my place, and I'll give you a painting," I said.

"Where did you get your talent from?" she said.

"My grandfather painted and played the piano. He's the only one in the family though. Everybody else is in business, which I hate. My mother is a teacher. I guess I took after her there. I taught English at the university for a few years. I like beauty, the beauty of language, colors, music," I said.

"Do you think I'm beautiful?" she said.

"I think you're hot, which is better than beautiful. You have a sense of humor. You're a cool chick."

"Thanks. You're a nice guy, too."

She made some coffee, and we sat at her small kitchen table. I felt comfortable with her, and I could tell she liked me.

"Do you have any children?" I asked.

"One. She's with her father right now. We're going through a custody battle. He drinks and uses drugs, so I'm hoping that will convince the judge that I can take better care of her. She's six, and so cute. You'd like her."

"Were you both using when she was conceived?"

"Yes, unfortunately. She seems perfectly normal though. She behaves in school and does pretty well. Who knows how she'll be when she grows up. Do you have any kids?"

"No. I was engaged once, but I pushed her away. Sometimes I regret it. She was very beautiful, but she didn't make me laugh. The sex was so good I thought I was in love."

"Sex always seems to complicate things, doesn't it?" she said.

"It's better to be good friends for a long time," I said.

"But I want to fuck you tonight," she said, laughing.

"I want to fuck you, too," I said, kissing her.

I grabbed her ass and shoved my tongue deep into her mouth.

"Maybe we should wait," she said. "Your girlfriend wouldn't like it."

"What my girlfriend doesn't know won't hurt her."

"Let's wait anyway," she said.

"Can we kiss?"

"Sure."

We kissed for a while and then talked some more.

"I'd better go home," I said.

"She's probably wondering where you are," Julie said.

"Why are you always bringing her up?"

"Because I'm jealous."

I left, and there were three messages from Jennifer. I called her and told her I had been at the hall the whole time and that I would call her in the morning. I couldn't sleep at all that night. I kept having cravings for pot and for sex with Julie. I imagined going back to rehab. Maybe it was the only thing that would work. I didn't want to go, but I couldn't think of anything else to do. I got about two hours of sleep in the morning and woke up angry. I didn't usually take out my frustrations on other people, but I yelled at Jennifer when I called her. She took it pretty well. She was very understanding, but I wasn't very proud of myself afterwards. We made up on the phone right away, and she wanted to meet me, so I went over to her place. When I got there, she was just getting out of the shower. I walked in and told her through the bathroom door that I was there. She came out in her robe and kissed me.

"Are you feeling better?" she said.

"Yeah, listen, I'm sorry I yelled at you. There was no reason for it."

"You already apologized. Forget about it."

"I'm having a lot of trouble controlling my emotions right now."

"You have to stay clean for a while before your emotions settle down," she said. "I know that much."

"Do you think I should go back to rehab?"

"I don't know. I think you can do it with just the meetings. You have to get past the first few days. I'm not the expert here.

Why don't you ask Gregory? He can give you the best advice."

I looked out the window with sad eyes. I wanted a year of sobriety right that minute and realized I was still angry at myself. I didn't think that I could really go to Italy, but at first I didn't say anything about it.

"I don't want to go back to rehab. I'm going to stick it out here at the meetings," I said.

"Good for you. I think you can do it," she said emphatically.

"I appreciate your support. You've been great. I know I've put you through a lot."

"We can still go to Italy in a month or two, can't we?" she said.

"We'll see."

She was silent for a long time, but not as if she were pouting, more like she was thinking hard. Perhaps she was imagining living in Italy and what it would be like there. I felt depressed and knew the next few weeks would be very difficult. Before, I was in a halfway house surrounded by people in recovery. Here I felt like I was one my own.

"Maybe we can go to Italy for a few weeks anyway," she said.

"That's a good idea. We can take a trip. That will get my mind off the pot. For now, we have to concentrate on your last papers and exams."

"I wish you would write part of that theory paper for me," she said.

"You know I can't do that."

"I know. I'm kidding."

"No, you're not."

"You're right. I'm sorry."

"It's no big deal, but you have to think these things through on your own," I said.

"You help me anyways. Can't you at least outline the paper for me?"

"No."

I was getting irritated. She was sounding like a daughter, or something. I wished she were older, but I knew she was maturing nicely. She was more mature than I was at that age.

"I'll do it, but you'll discuss it with me, won't you?"

"Sure."

"I have to go to class. Are you going to the hall?"

"Yes."

"I'll see you later," she said as she got dressed.

I drove to the hall and saw Gregory and Julie outside smoking. I was so glad to see them, I had a rush of excitement.

"Hey," I yelled out of the window of my car.

They waved, and I saw that Julie had a big smile on her face.

"How are you doing?" Julie said as I walked up to them.

"I'm still having a tough time."

"Hang in there," Greg said.

"I'm going to stick it out here in Syracuse. I'm not going to Italy, at least not for any extended period of time," I said.

"Good," Julie said with a smile.

"You two are becoming an item around here," Greg said.

"Are they talking about us?" Julie said, surprised.

"They talk even if nothing is going on," he said.

"Let them talk. It doesn't make any difference," I said.

"Maybe we'll give them something to talk about," she said, winking at me.

"I'm up for that," I said.

"Your girlfriend might not be too thrilled about that," Greg said.

"My girlfriend and I are probably going to split up," I said.

"Soon?" Julie said.

"Probably," I said.

"That's what they all say," Greg said.

"You don't know," Julie said.

"No, I don't," he said.

Greg could always see through me, no matter what was going on. He had a lot of experience and knew bullshit when he heard it. I wanted to get Julie into bed that day, but I wasn't too sure of how to go about it. The meeting started, and we all went inside. I brought up another topic and so did a woman I didn't know. I heard some good things and felt better afterwards. We went outside and smoked. A couple of guys that knew Greg introduced themselves to me. I was feeling more at home there all the time. I couldn't stop staring at Julie's ass as she talked to a young girl.

"What are you looking at?" Greg said.

"What do you think?" I said.

"I think you can have it if you want it," he said.

"I want it, but I don't want to get caught."

"No feelings of guilt? You just don't want to get caught. Is that it?" he said.

"That's it."

"I don't blame you. I'm jealous is all."

Julie came over to me after a while.

"Are you feeling better?" she said.

"A little bit," I said.

"Do you want to come over and have a salad with me?" she said.

"Sure, but why don't we go my house. I have some great things to eat."

"Okay."

Julie came over, and I showed her all my paintings, explaining in some detail the story behind each one. I also showed her a couple of my poems. She seemed impressed, and we got into an interesting conversation, while I made a fancy salad. I was curious about something, so I just came out and asked her.

"Did you ever have sex for money or drugs?" I said.

"Sure. How about you?"

"Not really, but I've slept with a prostitute a few times."

"That's the same thing."

"You're right. What about now? Would you accept money?"

"I guess I would if the price were right. But the price is much higher now. You have to understand how a poor girl like me gets by. We're not all related to wealthy families," she said. "Why? Were you thinking of paying me?"

"I don't want to do that."

"You don't have to," she said. "You can make a salad for me," she said, laughing.

We ate in silence for a while. I looked at her silky blonde hair and her crystal blue eyes, thinking how hot she was. I wanted to fuck her in the worst way, but I thought about how Jennifer would take it if she found out.

"Do you have big cock?" She laughed.

"Pretty big. Where did that come from?" I said, laughing.

"I'm only trying to keep the conversation interesting. You know we're going to fuck. It's only a matter of when."

"What about your preoccupation with my girlfriend?" I said.

"I'm not worried about it anymore."

"Do you want to fuck today?" I said.

"Maybe, but first I want to know if you're kinky at all."

"Not really. What about you?"

"A little," she said.

"Like what?"

"Oh, now I have your curiosity piqued. I like taking it up the ass," she said with a laugh.

"I like that, too, but that's not really kinky," I said.

"Yes, it is."

"Well, what else do you like? I was thinking about whips and chains."

"I like being tied up with silk scarves." She laughed.

"I don't think I have any silk scarves. How about a belt instead?"

"That will do."

"I'm getting horny just talking about it," I said.

"So am I," she said, as she came over to me and kissed me with passion.

We kissed for a while. She liked to make her tongue go in circles, while I thrusted mine in and out. After a few minutes, she unbuckled my belt and pulled my pants down. I was already hard when she began to suck on it. I was about to come, but I wanted to wait, so I lifted her head off me. I was thinking about fucking her up the ass and started taking her clothes off. We were on the couch in the living room, so I asked her if she wanted to move to the bedroom. She said no, the couch was fine. There we were, naked, with me trying to force my cock up her ass, when I heard the front door opening. Jennifer had come over and let herself in. She took one look at us and screamed, "Bastard!" and left.

Julie got up and put her clothes on. She was very apologetic, but I told her it was my fault.

"I hope I haven't ruined your relationship," Julie said softly.

"It was over with anyway," I lied.

"She might get over it," Julie said. "Maybe you should call her after I leave and tell her it was a one-time thing, and that it didn't mean anything."

"I like you, Julie. I don't want this to be a one-time thing."

"I like you too, Paul, but I don't want to come between the two of you."

"I need a more mature woman. Jennifer is too young for me, I think, and I like the fact that you're in recovery, too. You understand better what I'm going through," I said.

"We'll see," she said.

We drove over to the hall, where her car was parked, and I kissed her goodbye on the cheek.

I'll talk to you later," I said.

"I'm coming back here later. Why don't you come by?" she said.

"I will."

All the time, driving home, I thought about what I would say to Jennifer. I wanted to keep both relationships alive, because I didn't really know which one I liked better. I was confused and felt desperate. I called Jennifer as soon as I got home.

"Hello?" she said.

"Hi."

"What do you want?"

"I'm not sure what I want to say, but you have to believe me. I didn't plan that."

"Who is she?"

"A girl I met at the meeting."

"A whore, I suppose."

"Not really."

"Are you going to see her again?"

"No, definitely not."

"I can't see you for a while. I have to think about this. I'm very upset," she said.

"I understand. I'm sorry. I really am."

"Why would you jeopardize our relationship? Was it really worth it?"

"No, it was stupid."

"I'll talk to you later," she said, and hung up.

Now I felt like shit, and the first thing that entered my mind was to smoke pot. I thought about it for a minute, then I decided to call Greg.

"Hey, what's up?" he said.

"I did the most foolish thing possible."

"What was that, smoke?"

"No, I got caught fucking Julie by Jennifer."

"Was the most foolish thing the fact that you got caught, or doing it to begin with?"

"I shouldn't have done it but getting caught is even worse."

He started to laugh and kept laughing for a while. I thought it was a tragic situation, but he seemed to find some humor in it.

"Real funny," I said.

"If you hadn't got caught, you would be all right, wouldn't you?"

"Yeah, but now what am I going to do? I had two. Now I'll probably have neither," I said.

"Can't you be satisfied with one?" he said, laughing.

"Yes, but she has to be the right one."

"The grass is always greener…" he said.

"You're not helping me any."

"Pick one and stick with her," he said nervously.

"The problem is I can't pick."

"All this is driving you crazy, which makes it a whole lot

easier to pick up a drink or smoke pot."

"I know. That's all I think about."

I suddenly had another urge to smoke a joint, but I stayed on the phone with Greg until he talked me out of it. After I talked to Greg, I decided to go to the hall to see if I could run into Julie. She was outside smoking, and all I could think about was that plump ass.

"Hi," she said seriously.

"Listen, Julie, I'm sorry I put you through that. It'll never happen again."

"It's all right, but you must be pretty confused right about now."

"I am, of course, but I really like you. I'm thinking about dropping Jennifer. She's too young for me," I said.

"You're just saying that. I don't think you mean it."

"No, I'm serious. Would you still want to go out with me after what happened?"

"I don't know," she said slowly.

"I know what you're thinking…"

"You don't know what I'm thinking!"

"You're thinking that if I cheated on her, then I'll cheat on you," I said.

"That's not what I was thinking at all."

"Then what were you thinking?"

"Well, if you must know, that you don't have enough sobriety right now, and that you might take me back out," she said.

"But you weren't a pot smoker," I said.

"That doesn't make any difference."

"I'm doing a little bit better. Anyway, with your help, I think I can do it. I don't want to get high anymore."

62

"We'll see," she said.

"Do you want to get together tonight?" I said, almost sheepishly.

"You're relentless, aren't you?"

"I'm sorry."

"And quit apologizing," she said.

"Okay."

I felt like a fool, as I felt her slipping out of my grasp. I wasn't being my normal self, whatever that was, and I felt like an idiot.

"Don't pay any attention to me," I said.

"I know you're going through a tough time. I've been through it myself, but you can't expect me to follow you into hell."

"No. I guess we'd better cool it for a while, but I'd still like to spend time with you," I said.

"We can talk here, and you should talk to Greg more. He knows what's going on."

I thought about talking to Jennifer later. I had fucked that up pretty well.

"I'll see you later," I said to her, and left.

I was a mess. I wanted to get high and listen to jazz at home, escaping from everybody and everything. I knew my disease was one of isolation and escape, but I didn't care. I went home and called Greg again, who I figured was getting tired of me.

"Hey, what's up?" he said cheerfully.

"I went to a meeting, talked to Julie, and left before it started."

"You are a mess. I suggest you make the meetings and stay away from the women," he said.

"I can't. The women are too tempting," I said.

"They're part of your illness. You want to get better, don't you?" he said.

"Of course I want to get better, but I'm so lonely at home, and I don't have many new friends. I can't lock myself up in my house and do nothing!"

"You don't have to lock yourself up in your house. You can get a job, see new friends at the meetings, and lead the semblance of a normal life," he said.

I thought about it for a minute and saw that I had to make some serious changes. I decided to go to another meeting but only talk to the men.

"Sorry for bothering you again, Greg. You've been a true friend to me."

"No problem. You're helping me, too," he said.

After I hung up, I thought about calling Jennifer, but didn't. I made a sandwich for myself and drove back to the hall. I was so grateful that they had meetings all day long. I was determined to stay clean and sober, no matter what happened.

I was pleased to see Julie outside again. She didn't have that much time under her belt either, so she hung out at the hall a lot. My plans to talk only to the men quickly flew out the window.

"Hi," she said.

"Hi," I said. "I'm not going to apologize again. Don't worry."

"I wasn't worried."

"I've decided that it would be better for both of us if we only stayed friends," I said.

"I think that's a good idea. I'm not ready for another boyfriend either."

"I also think I'm going to break up with Jennifer."

"Oh, you don't have to do that. You two love each other.

That's rare."

"Yeah, but we fight a lot, and I need as much serenity as I can get."

"You need some stability in your life. She might be able to provide that for you," Julie said.

"You might be right," I said.

"Besides, I don't think you can live without any sex," she said with a laugh.

"You might be very right about that!" I laughed.

"More seriously, how bad are the cravings?"

"They're still pretty bad, but they seem to be subsiding all the time. At least now I know how to take my mind off them."

"I'd like to know how you do that," she said.

"I think about something else, like booze, or women, or food, anything but pot."

I knew she still had physical cravings from time to time as well, but it was the mental obsession that worried me the most. I was determined to sit through the next meeting, no matter how I felt. Julie looked so beautiful, and my mind went right to the moment I was going to plunge my cock into her ass. I thought about Jennifer and figured that I could probably patch things up with her again.

"I try to think about the future and how great I'm going to feel when the obsession goes away," she said.

"That's a great way to get over the cravings," I said. "I also think about how bad it was in the past and how good the present is."

"I try not to think about the past for too long," she said. "I've had many painful experiences."

"So have I," I said. "Let's go in. The meeting is about to start."

We sat together, and I was thinking about bringing up a topic, but I didn't. Julie seemed uncomfortable. She kept shifting in her seat. I tried to listen carefully, but I couldn't concentrate very well. They called on me, but I didn't say anything. I kept thinking about Jennifer and what I would say to her if I called her.

"Do you want to get out of here? You seem antsy," I whispered to Julie.

"Yeah, let's go get a cup of coffee somewhere," she said.

We walked out quietly and drove away in my car. I wanted to fuck her so bad, but I didn't say anything.

"I'm still uncomfortable in meetings," I said.

"So am I. All somebody has to say is that their life has been destroyed by drugs and alcohol, and I feel terrible."

We stopped at a local coffee shop and went inside. I sat near the window and thought for the first time in a long time about my friends in California. I felt bad for abandoning Laura there. She was a good kid, but I couldn't handle her immaturity.

"Are you really going to stop seeing Jennifer?" Julie said.

"I'm pretty sure I will. Why?"

"Because I'm lonely," she said, looking down.

"I'm lonely even if I'm with somebody," I said, smirking.

"I know that feeling, too," she said, "and I want something different."

"I like you, Julie. I want to be more than friends."

"I like you, too."

"Then let's go out with each other," I said.

"You have to break up with Jennifer first."

"Okay. But what about sleeping together?"

"I think we should wait a while," she said.

"That's probably a good idea, but I thought I didn't have enough sobriety," I said.

"If you go back to smoking pot, I'll leave you," she said.

"Maybe we'll inspire each other to stay sober," I said.

"You have to do it for yourself primarily," she said.

I sipped my coffee and looked into her sparkling blue eyes. I felt happy momentarily and wondered if we were making a good decision. I thought about what I'd say to Jennifer but figured that was already over with anyway.

Chapter 6

"Can we sleep together without having sex?" I said.

"What do you think?"

"I don't know. We could try it."

"I don't think it would work." She laughed.

"But I get so lonely sleeping alone," I said.

"So do I, but we shouldn't rush into this, if we're going to do it right."

"I want to sleep together," I whined.

"Cut it out," she said.

"Okay."

I looked at her and smiled.

"I can wait. It'll be worth it," I said.

We sipped our coffee in silence and looked at each other with loving eyes. I felt at ease with her, perhaps because we were in similar situations. Jennifer didn't understand very well, and I couldn't expect her to.

"Why don't you come over, and I'll sleep on the couch," I said.

"No. I'll sleep on the couch," she said.

"Then it's a deal. I promise I won't touch you," I said.

"I might touch you though," she said with a laugh.

"That's all right with me."

We drove back to the hall to pick up her car. Then we went back to my place. I made some coffee and turned on the stereo. I didn't watch much television. There was never anything on. We sat close together on the couch. After talking for only two minutes, we started kissing.

"We shouldn't," she said, pushing me away.

"Why not?"

"We already talked about this."

"We're going to end up making love sooner or later," I said.

"Well, then, let's make it later."

"Oh, come on, what's the big deal? We've already been naked together," I said.

"I thought you wanted this to work out."

"I do, of course, but what's a little fooling around?"

"I knew this would happen. I'd better go," she said.

"Don't go. I'll behave," I said.

"Are you sure?"

"Yes."

"Sit over there," she said.

I moved over on the couch and put my hands on my lap. It was getting dark out, and I was getting hungry.

"Do you want a sandwich? That's all I have," I said.

"Sure. What do you have?"

"Turkey."

"Perfect."

We ate our sandwiches, and all I could think about was fucking her in the ass. I turned on the television, and we watched some stupid movie. After about an hour, I leaned down and put my head in her lap. She stroked my hair, and I closed my eyes. I rolled over and put my face right in her crotch. I moved my tongue over her pants, and I could hear her moan. She spread her legs and pulled her pants down. I licked her and licked her, until I got tired. Then, finally, I fucked her up the ass. I came inside her and rolled over exhausted.

"That hurt a little," she said.

"I'm sorry. I won't push so hard next time," I said.

"Maybe we should use some jelly."

"Of course, I'll buy some," I said.

We decided to go to sleep early and went into the bedroom, which was a mess.

"I'll help you clean in the morning," she said.

"It's not usually this bad. I've been neglecting everything."

"I'm not going to be your mother."

"I don't want you to be. I already have a mother."

We slept pretty well together except I had a couple of violent dreams. I sweated through a t-shirt and got up in the middle of the night to change it. She slept all the way through the night. In the morning, I felt pretty good and got up to make coffee. We were still getting used to each other, but we were both trying to fit in together.

"I'll do the dishes. How long have they been in here?" she said.

"A few days."

"You need another mother."

"I need a wife."

"We'll talk about that some other time," she said.

"Let's talk about in now," I said.

"How can we get married? We only met a little while ago!"

"Like you said, I need some stability in my life, and you can provide that for me," I said.

She shook her head and grew silent for a minute.

"I appreciate the sentiment, Paul, but you're in no position to get married."

"I can support you," I said.

"I see you've given this some thought."

"I'm always thinking about marriage when I go out with somebody. Don't tell me it hasn't entered your mind," I said.

"It entered my mind."

"See."

"But that doesn't mean I'm going to jump right into it. I don't even know if I get along with you," she said.

"We would be great together, like all those couples in recovery. We could go to meetings together, take care of the children. It would be great!"

"Don't get so excited. We're just getting started. Let's see how things go," she said.

"Okay. I'm sorry. I feel good today is all."

"I feel good, too. It's almost time to go to the meeting," she said.

We took my car to the meeting. Gregory was outside smoking.

"I see you two have got together," he said.

"It was inevitable," I said.

"We're only having a little fun," Julie said.

"Yeah, a little fun. I've heard that before," he said.

"We're trying not to get too serious too quickly," I said.

"It's too late," Greg said. "What happened to your other girlfriend anyway?"

"She caught us in bed," I said with a laugh.

"I'm glad you think that's funny," he said with a chuckle.

"She's too young for him anyway," Julie said.

We went into the meeting and sat at our usual seats. There were quite a few people, and many that I recognized. I felt more comfortable this time, and it seemed that Julie did, too. When they asked people to share and went around the room, all I said was, "Keep a sense of humor."

Julie went on and on about all her fears, and I listened with intense curiosity. Greg didn't say anything, and besides, he was always his own problem. The meeting went pretty well. I felt better afterwards. I couldn't wait to get outside to smoke, and I lit up as soon as I got out the door. Julie smoked menthols, like Greg, so they often shared their cigarettes.

"I didn't realize you have so many fears," I said to Julie.

"You don't?" she said.

"I guess I do, too," I said.

"It's probably not as bad as I shared. Once I get talking, I can't stop," she said.

"We all have fears," Greg said. "It's natural."

"Some have more than others," Julie said.

"I'm afraid of relapsing," I said.

"That's a healthy fear," Greg said.

"I'm afraid of that, too," she said.

"Most of us in here are afraid of going back out. That's what keeps us here," he said.

"What exactly is fear anyway?" I said.

"It's a feeling, I guess," Greg said.

"But where does it come from?" I said.

"A response to the environment," Julie said.

"Or it could be completely irrational," I said.

"It can cripple a person. I know that," Greg said.

"A lot of people never do what they really want to do because of fear," she said.

"Yeah, women never ask men out, or call them the first time." I laughed at that.

"That's not true," Julie said.

"I never had much fear when I was smoking pot," I said.

"That's why a lot of us drink and use," Greg said, "to get

over some kind of fear."

"Is that why the fear is so intense when we get sober?" I said.

"Sure. The fear is heightened because the mask is gone. It levels off after a while though," Greg said.

"Well, it hasn't leveled off for me," Julie said.

"Me neither," I said.

We all decided to go our separate ways, and I told Julie I would hook up with her later. I was dreading going back to my apartment alone, so on the way, I decided to give Jennifer a call. I didn't know what to expect, but I didn't think it would be good. The apartment was much neater, which made me feel better. I called Jennifer.

"Hi," she said. "I still don't want to talk to you."

"Okay," I said, and hung up.

Now I felt horrible, and all I wanted to do was get high, but I didn't. I was taught to burn through these feelings, and I was determined to do so. I thought about how stupid I was and felt guilty, but I still didn't smoke. I spent the rest of the day watching TV and stewing in my own shit. I tried to sleep but couldn't. I tossed and turned all night and woke up feeling like hell. I called my mother first thing in the morning, after a couple of cups of hot coffee.

"Hi, sweetheart," she said. "How are you doing?"

"Not very well," I said. "I can't sleep. I think Jennifer has left me, and all I want to do is get high."

"Do you want to go back to rehab?" she said.

"I was thinking about it. What do you think?"

"Well, if you're feeling so bad, maybe the halfway house would be a good place for you for a few months," she said.

"Let me think about it," I said.

"Okay," she said.

After I talked to her, I felt so tired. I decided to take a nap. After about an hour in bed, I got a phone call from Greg.

"Hey, what's up? You didn't make it to the meeting this morning," he said.

"I had to get some sleep. I didn't sleep at all last night," I said.

"Then I know you didn't smoke," he said.

"No, I'm determined not to."

"Good! Are you going to the hall later?"

"Yeah, I'll try to make it at noon," I said.

"I'll meet you there," he said.

I tried to get more sleep but couldn't. I fried some eggs and bacon and ate, even though I wasn't hungry. At eleven thirty, I went to the hall and hung out until Greg arrived. He had a big grin on his face when he walked up.

"I forgot to ask you," he said, "how was Julie in bed?"

"She was great."

"Better than Jennifer?"

"Yeah, she has more experience."

"Experience is everything, but there is something to be said for a tight young body," he said.

Jennifer has a great tight ass," I said.

"Have you talked to her?" he said.

"She doesn't want to talk. I called her a few times," I said.

Julie pulled into the parking lot, and I could tell by her expression that she wasn't feeling too good. She walked very slowly toward us with her head bent down, and I was wondering what had happened.

"Hi. What's the matter?" I said.

"Nothing and everything," she said.

"It's not about us, is it?" I said.

"No, yes, who knows? I'm having a bad day," she said.

"You need a meeting," Greg said.

"You're not kidding. I woke up in the middle of a nightmare, and I'm still thinking about it. I have so much fear. I don't know where it's coming from. I was afraid to walk out my door this morning," she said.

"I had that fear, too," I said. "I was even afraid to drive sober, thinking I would get into an accident."

"It'll go away," Greg said.

"When?" she said.

"In a few months," he said.

"What's a few?" I said.

"It depends on the individual," he said. "It could be six, or nine, or twelve, but you're going to have to be patient."

"That's something I don't have much of," she said.

"That'll come, too," he said.

The meeting began and fortunately it wasn't too crowded. I liked the smaller meetings because it was easier to talk and I could express my feelings for a longer period of time. The three of us sat together, and Gregory leaned back, crossing his legs. I was thinking how nice it would be to be so relaxed. When it came my time to speak, I shared about how difficult it was to socialize with "normal" people, and how much more comfortable I felt with other alcoholics. After the meeting, the three of us went out and smoked.

"That was a good meeting," Julie said.

"It's amazing how they make you feel so much better, at least for a while," I said.

"You'll see in a couple of years that you'll feel good most of the time," Greg said.

"Won't that be nice," she said, "but I still have to do some homework, like a resentment inventory."

"And sex," I said.

"Yours should be interesting," she said.

"Not as interesting as yours," I said.

"What's that supposed to mean," she said.

"Nothing. I was only kidding. Don't be so sensitive," I said.

"I can't help it. I'm having a bad day," Julie said.

"My sex inventory was pretty interesting," Greg said.

"I bet," I said.

"I had a lot of lovers," he said.

"It's quality that counts," Julie said.

"That's right," I said.

"I had quality, too," Greg said, "and lots of it."

"I have a big resentment against my father," Julie said.

"What did he do?" I said.

"He physically and verbally abused me," she said.

"Did he molest you?" Greg asked.

"No. At least he didn't do that. My mother would have killed him," she said.

"No wonder you got into drugs," I said. "I have no excuse. I had a great childhood, and my parents are not alcoholics."

"How did you get into it?" Greg said.

"I went to college," I said, laughing. "No, not really. I had some sort of nervous breakdown and self-medicated for a few years."

"I think I'm having a nervous breakdown today," Julie said.

"You're not," I said. "You only think you are."

"Are you on medication?" Greg asked Julie.

"Yes. I'm on an antidepressant and a drug for anxiety," she said.

"Are they helping?" he said.

"Not today. I feel like getting high," she said.

"That won't help anything," I said.

"I have to take off," Greg said. "Why don't we meet here later?"

"Okay," Julie and I said.

We hung out for a while, and I asked her if she wanted to come over to my place.

"Sure, for a little while," she said.

We drove to my house in separate cars, and I noticed for the first time that it was a beautiful sunny day. It occurred to me that I was far too self-absorbed and that I needed to be less self-conscious. When I pulled into the driveway, all I could think about was fucking Julie.

"What do you have to eat? I'm starving," she said.

"I can make you a BLT."

"That would be great."

After we ate, we lay down on the couch to take a nap. Neither of us was sleeping well, so we took naps. I couldn't sleep next to her though. I was too horny. I started kissing her, and she was into it. Pretty soon I had my hand down her pants and was rubbing her clit. She bit my lower lip and forced her tongue into my mouth. I sucked on her tongue for a while, keeping my finger working on her clit.

"Oh, that feels so good!" she said.

"I want to fuck you up the ass," I said.

"I want to suck your cock," she said.

I pulled down my pants and put my cock in her mouth, holding my body above her. I got tired after a while, so we changed positions. I lay down on my back, and she kneeled next to the couch, continuing to suck me. I almost came, so I pushed her head away.

"Fuck me," she said.

I put my arms through her legs and lifted her knees up to her head. She helped me in, and I thrust slowly for a while, making her moan. Then I picked up speed, and she began to scream. Suddenly, I flipped her over and lifted her ass into the air. I slowly put my very hard cock into her ass and pushed until I was all the way in.

"Easy," she said.

"I should use the jelly, shouldn't I?"

"Please."

I got up and walked into the bedroom to get the jelly. She was on all fours waiting for me. I lubed her ass with my finger and greased myself all up. When I put it back in, it slid easily in and out. It was so stimulating I came quickly, and it felt so good.

"Ohhh!" I said.

"You like that, don't you?" she said.

"You like it, too, don't you?" I said.

"Sure, but I can't come that way," she said.

"Why don't you rub your clit while I fuck you," I said.

"I'll try that next time."

I held her close to me, and we finally fell asleep. We slept for about an hour and talked when we got up.

"Do you really like me?" she said.

"Of course I do. What makes you ask that?"

"I don't know. I'm very insecure these days," she said.

"If I make love to you, it means I like you," I said.

"I've heard that before. You've probably fucked a lot of women you didn't care for," she said.

"A couple, I guess, but I've grown out of that. I'm looking for a woman whom I can truly love," I said.

"Don't use that word."

"I didn't say I was in love with you, but that's what I'm looking for, and I wouldn't be spending all this time with you if I didn't care," I said.

"I appreciate that," she said.

"Let's go to the hall," I said.

"Good idea."

We got in our cars and drove to the meeting hall. It was late afternoon, and there weren't too many people there. The sun was out, and there was a light breeze. A meeting was about to start, but we stood out on the lawn and smoked.

"I could fall in love with you," she said.

"Same here, but let's take our time for a change," I said.

"We've already slept together. What do you mean take our time?" she said.

"Let's not say the love word for a while," I said.

"That's fine with me," she said.

I thought about Jennifer and how I had always told her that I loved her. I did feel very strongly about her, but I knew love meant a certain commitment that I wasn't willing to make yet.

"I only said that I could fall in love with you," she said.

"Well, I could fall in love with you, too, but I don't want to make any promises, knowing my track record."

"I'm not looking for a promise, only a feeling of respect and compassion," she said.

"You have that," I said.

At that moment, Greg showed up.

"Hey, what's up?" he said. "Are you feeling any better, Julie?"

"A little, but Paul is giving me a hard time," she said.

"I am not," I said.

"You two might want to cool it for a while. Neither of you is very stable," he said.

"We're trying to keep things in perspective," I said.

"Some perspective," she said.

"Take it easy now. You might want to spend a little less time together and get to know some other people," he said.

"That's a good idea," I said.

"I agree," she said.

We went into the meeting, and I felt pretty good, considering all the bullshit that was going on in my life. I sat quietly and listened to everybody, even though my mind kept wandering. Julie shared about her anger and resentment toward her father, and I simply passed. It was a good meeting for both of us, and Greg was so used to them it hardly made any difference to him.

Chapter 7

We went out for coffee afterwards, and Gregory and Julie got into a heated debate.

"You have to let your resentments go," Gregory said.

"I can't simply let them go," Julie said.

"They're the most dangerous feelings for us. You're going to have to do something about them," he said.

"But I can't even talk to my father," she said.

"You have to pray for him then," he said.

"That'll be the day," she said.

"What about therapy?" he said.

"I tried that. It didn't work,"

"I give up," he said.

"Why don't you bring up the topic a few times and see what kind of response you get," I said.

"I'll try that," she said. "It's been eating me alive for years."

"I can't even imagine having a long-term resentment against my father. I forgave him a long time ago," I said.

"I'm more worried about my parents having resentments against me," Greg said.

"I try to concentrate on the love I get from my mother," Julie said.

"That's a good thing to do," I said.

"Are your parents still together?" Greg asked.

"No, they were divorced a couple of years ago," she said. "Now my mother has a boyfriend."

"What's he like?" I said.

"Fortunately, he's kind and sweet, unlike my father."

"I'm glad you have a good role model now," I said.

"I don't need a role model now," she said.

"I think we always need parental role models," Greg said.

"I agree," I said.

"I guess you're right," she said. "I'm glad my mother is finally happy."

We sipped our coffee in silence for a while, and I noticed that Julie still seemed disturbed. Gregory was perfectly relaxed, leaning back in his chair with his hands on his head. I was thinking about my mother, whom I considered a saint. She had let me go through my disease as though I had planned it, and then was right there for me when I needed to go to rehab. My father supported me as well, and over the years we had become very close.

"I think my fears stem from my father's abuse," Julie said.

"I'm sure," Greg said, "and like I said, the only way you're going to get over your resentment and fears is through therapy."

"I guess you're right. I'm going to have to try it again, this time sober and clean."

"You're going to feel so much better," I said.

"I need a good doctor, because I think I would benefit from some medication, like an antidepressant, or an anxiety drug," she said.

"That should be looked into," Greg said. "I take a medication."

"So do I," I said.

"You were probably self-medicating," Greg said to Julie.

"I know I was," she said.

"One can self-medicate with other things, like gambling, or

sex, or food," I said.

"I'm not worried about all that right now," she said.

"One thing at a time," Greg said.

We decided to go our separate ways and meet again later. I went to the grocery store and bought a lot of food that I could freeze, since my hours were not regular enough to cook fresh food. I called everybody in my family when I got home, and they were all glad I was hanging in there. My parents were very supportive, and they always asked if there was anything they could do for me. I took a nap after dinner and got a surprise call from Jennifer.

"Hey," she said.

"I'm glad you called," I said.

"I've been thinking."

"Yes."

"I've decided to forgive you," she said.

"Good."

"On one condition," she said.

"What's that?"

"I want you to be faithful to me," she said.

"I can't promise that," I said.

"Then forget it," she said, and hung up.

I could have lied to her, but I didn't feel like it. I was starting to get attached to Julie and was willing to let Jennifer go. I still wanted to fuck Jennifer, but my life was too complicated. I decided to go back to the hall to meet Julie and Greg. I was still having cravings, but the meetings made them more manageable. When I got to the hall, Julie and Greg were on the lawn, smoking. She was wearing a tight pair of jeans and a top that came above her navel. She looked really sexy.

"Hi, guys," I said.

"I called a psychiatrist," Julie said.

"Good," I said. "The meetings are not a cure-all."

"I made an appointment for tomorrow, and my insurance covers the whole thing," she said.

"Great," I said. "You sound better this evening."

"Yeah, talking to Greg really helped, and I took a nap, which was good."

"What did you do besides taking a nap that made you feel better?" Greg said.

"I actually prayed for my father," she said.

"You took a suggestion. That's rare for us," he said.

"I thought it was crazy, but it really worked!"

"Now you can pray for me," I said.

"I do that already," she said.

The meeting began, and everybody started to file in. After the three of us sat down, I noticed a young woman sit next to Greg. She was pretty cute, and Greg seemed to know her well. The meeting went okay, but I still didn't feel very comfortable. Afterwards, we went outside, and Greg introduced Lisa to us. Lisa had short dark hair, was about five feet five and had a nice figure. She looked to be about thirty-five.

"I don't usually come to this meeting," Lisa said. "I need to, but I have a few bad experiences with some guys."

"They're all vultures," Julie said and laughed as she looked at me.

"Don't look at me," I said. "I don't even like women!"

"Be careful when you say that!" Greg said, laughing.

"Why did you come today then? I'm curious," I said.

"I came to see Greg. We used to see a lot of each other," Lisa said.

"We're becoming good friends," I said.

84

"To tell the truth, I broke up with my boyfriend recently, and I'm on the prowl," Lisa said, looking at Greg.

"Maybe we should leave you two alone then," I said. "It was nice meeting you, Lisa. Maybe we'll see you tomorrow."

"I hope so," Lisa said.

Julie and I decided to go to her apartment, which I had never seen before. It was very nicely decorated, considering she had little money. She made some coffee, and we sat on the couch.

"No sex tonight," Julie said.

"What made you say that?" I said.

"I don't know. It seems that we always end up in bed, and I don't want to base our relationship on that," she said.

"I understand, but that's not why I like you," I said.

"I know, but I have a lot of self-doubt," she said.

"What do you want to talk about then?" I said.

"Why don't you tell me about your father and mother," she said.

"Well, my father is a very intelligent man, and he is extremely well read. He reads two newspapers a day, and some business magazines. He has never been drunk in his life, but once in a while enjoys a glass of wine. He likes to garden and is very close to his second wife. My mother is also very intelligent and likes to read, too. She was remarried but got divorced a second time. She loves to travel and now has a house in Florida. She walks every day and swims. Both my father and mother have a sense of humor, but mine is more like my father's," I said.

"Very interesting," she said.

"Tell me about your mother," I said.

"She's a nurse and quite good at it. She spent many nights at the hospital, so we were left with my father a great deal. She likes to read, garden, and watch movies," she said.

85

"What did your father do?"

"He had a small construction company," she said, "and he was always angry."

"My father has a temper, too, but he mixed it up with laughter," I said.

We started to kiss after talking for a while, and it wasn't long before we were naked. We made love, and I felt more emotional about it this time. I only thought about her. Jennifer didn't come into my mind. We went to sleep, and for the first time in a long time, I slept through the night. I felt her get up several times, but she didn't really wake me.

"Let's take a shower together," I said in the morning.

"Okay, but I don't want you to hog all the water," she said, laughing.

We got in the shower, and she soaped my cock with her hands. I fucked her from behind as I massaged her clit.

"You're driving me crazy!" she screamed.

"Now this is the way to start a day!" I said.

"Why is it that I always get naked with you?" she said.

"You can't resist me," I said.

"Let's eat something and go to the meeting," she said.

We had some eggs and bacon and went to the meeting in separate cars. Gregory was outside smoking.

"Hey, what's up?" he said.

"Another day in paradise," Julie said.

"You're feeling a lot better," he said.

"I'm having a calming influence on her, I think," I said.

"These meetings are really working," she said. "I'm starting to let a lot of things go."

"Good, keep it up," he said.

We went inside and sat down, and again Lisa sat next to

Gregory. She had a nice dress on and was wearing makeup. I still felt a little uncomfortable, but I was getting better. Lisa whispered something into Greg's ear, but I couldn't hear it. After a while, it was Julie's turn to speak.

"I'm starting to let go of my resentment toward my father, but at the same time, the more I think about it, the less respect I have for my mother. She stayed with him for so long, and he was nothing but abusive toward her and me. What makes a person stay in such an abusive relationship? I guess I'm still angry, and I don't know if I'll even be able to let that anger go," she said, then added, "That's all. Thanks for letting me share."

Then it was my turn.

"My cravings are slowly going away, and I have more peace of mind. I heard somebody in here say that peace of mind is the most sought-after thing for a human being, and I'm starting to believe that. I don't want any more chaos in my life. I want simplicity. That's all I have, thanks," I said.

Greg said: "My life is going more smoothly now. I was always my worst enemy, but I've learned to treat myself better. I have the love and respect of my family, which I never thought I'd have, and I'm pretty happy. That's all."

It was Lisa's turn, and I had never heard her speak.

"I used to put myself down all the time, like I'm not pretty enough, or smart enough, or I don't have any friends, or I don't laugh enough, but I've stopped doing that. Gregory told me to change tapes in my brain and tell myself that I'm a good and loving person. He's helped me turn my attitude around, one of the few things we can change in our lives. Thanks," she said.

I was impressed, and I told myself that she was really a great person. She spoke with a calm, self-assured voice, and as it turned out, she had healthy sense of humor. After the meeting, we went outside to find the sun shining.

"I'm surprised you used to tell yourself you aren't pretty enough," Julie said to Lisa. "You're beautiful."

"No, I'm not, but thank you. You're the one who is beautiful," Lisa said.

"I'm not nearly as pretty as you," Julie said.

"You gals are unbelievable," Greg said. "You need a dose of self-confidence."

"You're both beautiful," I said.

"Thanks," they said at the same time.

"I have to go to the doctor's," Julie said.

"I'll meet you at my house later," I said.

The women took off, while Greg and I smoked and talked.

"She's hot," I said.

"Yeah, I've known Lisa for a long time. She keeps getting into these bad relationships," he said.

"Same with Julie. I think it's a problem of self-esteem," I said.

"It's their parents' fault," Greg said.

"Why would anyone want to berate their kid until they have no sense of worth?" I said.

"Most of these parents are alcoholics or drug addicts themselves. They don't make the best parents," he said. "Many in the family have chemical imbalances that alter behavior."

"I'm lucky. I don't come from an alcoholic family. I'm the only one," I said.

"My grandfather was an alcoholic," he said, "but he functioned a lot better than I do."

"You function pretty well. Your mind is still sharp," I said, "and you're a big help to others."

"I try to do what I can. I had a lot of people help me. That's for sure," he said.

"Did you stay clean in prison?"

"Most of the time, but I fucked up there, too," he said.

"I don't know if I could stay clean in prison," I said.

"A lot of people there smoke pot at least," he said. "The trick for me was getting books to read."

"That's what I would have done, too, as well as write. Some of the best authors have been in prison," I said.

"I was thinking of writing a book," Greg said.

"I could help you," I said.

"That would be great," he said.

"You have a lot of interesting stories to tell," I said.

"I haven't even told you the hairiest ones," he said.

"Listen, I've got to go home and do some work. I'll meet up with you later," I said.

Chapter 8

When I went home, I sat down to do some writing, but couldn't concentrate. I was still thinking about Jennifer and Julie, and after hesitating for a while, called Jennifer.

"Hi," I said.

"Do we have anything to talk about?" she said.

"I think I can be faithful," I said.

"You think?"

"I know I can," I said.

"What about that woman?" she said.

"She's not in my life any more," I said.

"Good! I'm willing to try again if you are," she said.

"Great!"

"I have to go to class. I'll talk to you later."

Then I called Julie.

"Hey," I said.

"What's up, handsome?" she said.

"Nothing."

"Why don't we go for a drive in the country?" she said.

"That's a good idea. Why don't you make a couple of sandwiches, and I'll pick you up in a little while."

After I hung up, I felt like a real asshole. I couldn't commit to either one and I couldn't be alone. I didn't feel comfortable in my own skin, and I was looking for someone else to make me feel better. Greg had told me that I would feel this way for a while, but that didn't make me like it. I went over to pick up Julie.

It was a beautiful day, and my car was in good shape. We decided to drive up to a local lake and sit by the water.

"What's up? You're acting a little funny," she said.

"I don't know. I feel a bit weird is all."

"Did you get enough sleep?" she said.

"That's not it," I said.

We found a nice spot and put down a blanket. The air was fresh, and there were a few other people around.

"Have you called Jennifer lately?" she asked.

"Why do you ask that?" Of course not," I said.

"I don't know. You're acting funny is all."

"Well, that's not the reason," I said."

"What is it then?" she said.

"I think it's early recovery. I'm on an emotional rollercoaster."

"So am I, but I don't act funny," she said.

"What do you mean by funny?"

"You're not saying much, and when you do, you don't sound like yourself."

I lay back on the blanket and looked up at the sky. I didn't want to say anything for fear of sounding weird, but I didn't want to be silent either.

"I don't feel like my normal self today," I said.

"You can talk to me," she said.

"I don't really feel like talking," I said.

"Something specific is bothering you. I can sense it," she said.

"Stop nagging me."

"I'm not nagging."

"Can't we lie here and enjoy the beauty quietly?"

"Of course. I won't say another word," she said.

"Don't be upset. I'm sorry," I said.

"No. I know how you feel."

"I did talk to Jennifer," I said.

"I knew it. Why?"

"She called and wanted to be friends, which I said was fine."

"I've heard that story before," she said.

"No, I'm serious. We're not going out any more," I said.

"Well, then, don't be friends. You know women and men can't be friends after they've been involved," she said.

"Why can't mature men and women be friends?" I said.

"You have too much history," she said.

"Don't be jealous."

"I'm not jealous," she said.

I was silent for a while. I didn't want to upset her any more than she was. The sun beat down on us, but there was a breeze, so it wasn't too hot. I felt like a jerk, and she could sense it.

"Let's go," she said finally. "I have an appointment with the shrink."

I drove her home and tried to kiss her, but she wouldn't let me. When I got home, I turned on the TV and stared at it. I tried calling Jennifer again, but she wasn't home. I was stuck with myself. A lot of different thoughts ran through my head, none of them good. I wanted to smoke a joint but didn't have anything. I decided to call Gregory.

"Hey," I said.

"What's up, lover?"

"I'm not doing very well in that department," I said.

"What's the matter?"

"I called Jennifer and told her I would be faithful. Then I went out with Julie. Now Julie's mad because I told her I called Jennifer."

"You're making a mess of things aren't you?" he said.

"The problem is all I want to do is smoke pot."

"You've got to simplify your life and quit dating two women," he said.

"I can't help myself."

"Of course you can. What's the matter with you?"

"I don't know. I'm a jackass," I said.

"That's not a good explanation. Now if you want the cravings to go away, you have to do some work. Start doing some reading and drop one of the women," he said.

"I've been doing some reading. That I'm good at," I said.

"Now you have to do the hard part," he said.

"I like both of them," I said.

"I'm only giving you advice. You don't have to follow it if you don't want to," he said.

"I'll think about it," I said.

"That's all I'm asking you to do," he said.

"I'll talk to you later," I said.

As soon as I hung up, I felt confused again. I thought about what he'd said and decided to break up with Jennifer. The sex was so good though, I didn't know if I could. I didn't understand why I was so obsessed with sex, but I was. I took a short nap, and when I got up, called Jennifer again.

"Hi," she said.

"How was class?"

"Difficult."

"Do you want me to help you with your work?" I said.

"Would you?"

"Sure. I'll be right over."

I put on some clean clothes and drove over to her house. All I could think about was eating her tasty pussy. When I arrived, she was already studying.

"Will you read this article and tell me what you think?" she said.

"Sure."

I read the article and gave her my opinion.

"My question is: "If you can't know the present, how is the past unforgettable?"

"Interesting point. What does the word 'know' mean?" she said.

"I guess the experiences and concepts one can remember," I said.

"How do we know the present then?"

"It makes an immediate impression on our memory," I said. "Then it changes as it echoes."

"So, the present is never the same twice or again?" she said.

"That's right," I said. "You see, language is in motion, just like the present is in motion, and it registers in different ways, sometimes quickly, sometimes more slowly."

"I don't understand that very well," she said.

"I don't either. I don't know if anybody does," I said.

"What can we know, then?" she said.

"I know that God doesn't exist," I said. "That informs my entire way of living."

"How do you know that?"

"Because there's evil," I said.

"But there's beauty and goodness, too," she said.

"That's true, but that doesn't mean there's a God," I said.

"What else can we know?" she said.

"Well, I know that pure repetition is impossible, because the original and the copy cannot coincide in time and space," I said. "And I know that one without laughter is oppressed."

"These are all constants then?" she said.

"I believe so," I said.

"You're so smart," she said.

"And you are, too," I said.

Now that we had done some work, I went back to thinking about sex. I didn't want to upset her, but I wanted to kiss her and see where that led. I kissed her on the cheek.

"Is that all you think about?" she said.

"No, but we got our work done."

"I don't feel like doing anything," she said.

"Are you still mad?" I said.

"A little, maybe."

"Let it go, honey. I'm sorry. I truly am," I said.

"You have no morals," she said.

"What?"

"You heard me," she said.

"Why do you say that?" I said.

"You cheated on me."

"We're not even married," I said.

"You still cheated on me," she said.

"I said I was sorry."

"Well, it's going to take some time before I get over it," she said.

"I understand that," I said.

I decided it was time to go home before the argument got too heated. She was making me feel very uncomfortable, and I didn't want to smoke or drink over it.

"I'll call you in the morning," I said.

"All right," she said. "I'm sorry I said you have no morals. You're a sweet and loving guy."

"Thanks," I said, and left.

I went home to relax and sat in front of the TV. I was supposed to go to a meeting later that evening but didn't feel like it. I wanted to try feeling more comfortable by myself. I tried to read but ended up in front of the TV again. I couldn't relax. I decided to call Julie.

"Hey, what's up?" she said.

"You sound glad to hear from me," I said.

"I had a talk with the doctor, and he made me feel better. He prescribed me some medication. He said it would take about a week to start working. Are we going to the meeting tonight?"

"I guess so. I mean I don't really feel like it, but I suppose I should," I said.

"Come on. I'll meet you there," she said.

I ate something and drove to the hall. Gregory and Julie were already there.

"Hey," I said.

"You'd better keep an eye on this girl before I steal her away," Greg said.

"By the way, where's Lisa?" I said.

"She'll be here soon," he said.

"Here she comes now," Julie said.

Lisa parked her car and joined our little group.

"What's up, girl?" I said.

"Oh, one of the other nurses was giving me a hard time today. I hate that hospital. I'm going to find somewhere else to work."

"I bet you're a good nurse," Julie said.

"She's the best," Greg said.

"Thanks, but I'm only an LPN. I'm still studying to become an RN," Lisa said.

"You're good with people though. I can tell," I said.

"Some people are impossible to deal with though. They don't feel good, and they're not at their best," Lisa said.

"How long have you been in recovery?" Julie asked.

"A little over five years. I started when I was twenty-eight," she said.

"Good for you," I said.

"I met Greg the day I came in," Lisa said.

"I bet he was all over you," I said, laughing.

"I liked her from the start," Greg said.

"I think I'm going to bring up a topic tonight," Julie said.

"What about?" I said.

"Anger and fear. I think my anger is fear-based, but I don't feel the fear when I feel angry," she said.

"Then how do you know it's fear-based?" Greg said.

"Aren't most emotions fear-based?" Lisa said.

"I don't see that," I said.

"They might be mingled though," Julie said.

"I suppose there's a certain amount of instinctive fear," Greg said, "but when you feel love, you don't feel fear, do you?"

"Fear of rejection? Maybe," Lisa said.

"Not necessarily," I said.

"There might be a layer of fear underlying everything as an instinct to survive," Julie said.

"Well, there could be. We don't really know everything that's in our subconscious," Greg said.

"But how does that relate to your anger?" I said.

"I'm not sure. That's why I'm bringing it up," Julie said.

"What are you angry about?" Lisa said.

"I don't think I'm angry about a specific thing. I'm angry about everything," Julie said.

"What are you fearful about?" Greg asked.

"A lot of things, again, nothing specific," Julie said.

"Both of those will go away with time," Greg said.

"I feel awkward a lot," Julie said.

"That's normal for early recovery," Lisa said. "You have to burn through it."

We went into the meeting and sat in the back of the room. Julie brought up her topic and got more support than real answers. I shared that no matter how badly I felt, I could not pick up a drink or a drug. This was not news to anybody else, but I had to remind myself. After the meeting, we went to a coffee shop and hung out.

"What's Marv's problem?" Julie asked, referring to someone at the meeting.

"He's always depressed and angry," Lisa said. "One day I suggested to him that he get on some medication, and he snapped at me, so I haven't talked to him since."

"Some of those people have some very serious problems," Greg said.

"I'd hate to live like that," Julie said.

"You have no idea how good you're going to feel in a few months," Lisa said.

"That's good to hear," I said.

"Did some of your anger or fear go away?" Greg said to Julie.

"Yes, I feel better," she said.

"Those meetings work like magic," Lisa said.

"I feel better by sitting back and listening," I said.

"Do you still feel fear, Greg?" Julie said.

"When I'm trying to do something new," he said.

"But you still do it, don't you?" Julie said.

"Sometimes I shy away. I'll admit it," he said.

"I'm afraid to go back to teaching," I said.

"Why?" Lisa said.

"I don't know if I can do it anymore," I said.

"I'm sure you can," Julie said. "At least you're able to write and paint. I'm afraid of going back to school."

"I was afraid of going to school, too, but after the first few weeks, I got used to it," Lisa said.

"I went back to school, too," Greg said, "but I didn't finish."

"I have a Master's, but I wanted to get my Ph.D.," I said.

"You're probably not afraid to do that," Lisa said.

"A little," I said.

We talked for another hour. It seemed that nobody wanted to go home. Amazingly, my cravings had not appeared that night. I drove home and went straight to bed. There was a message from Jennifer. She was wondering where I was. It took me a few hours to go to sleep, but finally I dozed off and slept uninterrupted until morning.

When I awakened, I felt pretty refreshed and called my mother after having a cup of coffee.

"Hi, honey," she said. "How are you feeling?"

"Much better today. I don't know why."

"Glad to hear it. I'm playing bridge today. Then tonight I'm going to a movie."

"Good. I called to say that I'm feeling better, and that I'm going to stay off the pot. I'm going to a meeting after I shower," I said.

"Good. I'll talk to you later," she said.

After my shower, I called Jennifer.

"Hey, what's up?" I said.

"Nothing. I'm getting ready for class."

"Do you want to get together later?" I said.

"Sure. I'll call you," she said.

I was turned off by her tone of voice. She didn't seem too enthusiastic to talk to me. The first thought that entered my head was that she had found somebody else. I wasn't usually the jealous type, but it occurred to me. I went to the meeting and found Julie and Greg. Apparently, Lisa had gone to work.

"Hey," I said.

"You sound depressed," Greg said.

"Not really. I felt good in the morning. Now I feel kind of blah," I said.

"That happens. You might feel better after the meeting," Julie said.

"You sound pretty good," I said to Julie.

"Yeah, you know those antidepressants aren't supposed to work for a week, but I feel better already," she said.

"It depends on the person," Greg said. "When I started on them, it took two weeks."

"Do you know that a quarter of the population suffers from depression?" I said.

"Really? It's that high? No wonder so many people self-medicate," Julie said.

"I don't have that problem though," I said. "I'm on the manic side."

"You've got the good problem," Greg said.

We went into the meeting, and I noticed there weren't too many people. Julie brought up the topic of depression, or mood swings, and got some good feedback. I shared that I was having early recovery mood swings as well, but that I wasn't getting severely depressed. Greg shared that he had leveled off a long time ago, and that he was trying to maintain a healthy attitude. After the meeting, we went out and smoked.

"Is it possible to get more depressed after a meeting?" I said.

"Sure," Greg said. "Why? Is that how you're feeling?"

"A little hopeless, I guess," I said.

"You're the one with all the positive feedback," Julie said.

"I wasn't feeling that way during the meeting," I said.

"I think you're a little dishonest about your feelings," Julie said.

"No, I'm not. Besides, this is not a therapy session," I said.

"It's like therapy, but you're a teacher. I suppose you have to project a certain amount of confidence," Julie said.

"I was told not to whine and complain," I said. "I'm going home and try to do some work."

"See you later," Greg said.

"Bye, sweetheart," Julie said. "I hope I didn't hurt your feelings."

"No, I'm fine."

When I went home, I crashed from all the caffeine I had drunk. I took a nap and was interrupted by a phone call. It was Jennifer.

"Hi," I said.

"I need your help again," she said, laughing.

"I should charge you for this," I said.

"Can I come over?"

"Sure," I said.

I made some tomato soup with cheese in it, and when she arrived, we sat down to eat. I came to the simple realization that I was in love with two women. When I was with Jennifer, I experienced the excitement of being with a young, beautiful woman. When I was with Julie, I enjoyed being with a mature, experienced woman. Jennifer and I discussed some of her schoolwork, and afterwards jumped in bed.

"Let's do something different," I said.

"Like what?"

"I don't know. We always make love the same way," I said.

"You like coming in my mouth," she said.

"I know, but we can do some different things before the grand finale," I said.

"You tell me what to do, and I'll do it," she said.

We fumbled around for a while and discovered a new position. She was on her side, and I was behind her. This position allowed for deep penetration and was very pleasurable.

"How does that feel?" she said.

"Great."

"You can speed up if you want to."

"I like it slow likes this," I said.

We took our time, and it turned out to be the best lovemaking we had ever done. I fell back, exhausted.

"Let's go again," she said.

"Are you kidding? It's going to take me two hours to recover."

I took another nap, and she went into the living room to watch TV. I dreamed of getting into an argument with Julie and woke up with a start. I didn't feel too comfortable after that dream, and Gregory's words haunted me. I took a shower and joined Jennifer in the living room.

"I have to study. I'm going home," she said.

"I'm going to another meeting," I said.

When I got to the hall, Julie and Lisa were outside smoking. It was warm but cloudy. I knew Gregory would be there shortly. I didn't realize it at that time, but I was beginning to rely on Gregory for support. The women were only making it more difficult.

"Hey, what's up, stranger," Julie said.

"Nothing, I guess. My life seems to revolve around this hall. I'm glad you guys are here," I said.

"I used to come here all the time, too," Lisa said. "After a while you get a life."

"I need to go back to work," I said.

"I'm going back to school, I've decided," Julie said.

"Good for you. I'll help you," I said.

"I'll help you, too," Lisa said.

"What are you going to study?" I said.

"Well, I have to get my GED first, which involves English and math. Then I want to study psychology," Julie said.

"I studied a lot of psychology," Lisa said. "It's fascinating."

"I want to know more about how my own mind works," Julie said.

Gregory showed up at that moment, and I saw Lisa's face light up.

"Hi, honey," she said to him.

"What's going on, gang?" he said.

"Julie's going back to school," I said.

"Beautiful! See, we can get over our fears," he said.

"Well, I'm not over my fears, but I'm going to do it anyway," Julie said.

"Everybody is afraid to go back to school," I said.

"Everybody is afraid to do anything that is a real challenge," Lisa said, "but the rewards of accomplishing it are great."

"Sobriety is the hardest challenge I've ever faced," I said.

"It's not easy," Greg said.

We chatted for quite a while, and I felt pretty comfortable with my new friends. I thought about Jennifer and suddenly felt like a jerk. I had to resolve this issue soon and finally pick one.

We went into the meeting, and my comfortability disappeared. I brought up the topic of being on edge most of the time and discovered that everybody else had felt the same way in early sobriety. My cravings were subsiding slightly, but sometimes they were intense. I felt better sitting next to Julie, knowing that she understood everything I was going through. Greg shared that his mental obsession had taken him out time after time, long after the physical cravings had passed. Afterwards, we hung out with several of the others.

"I'm starting to feel better in the meetings," Julie said. "I don't know if it's the antidepressants or what."

"After a while, you start to really enjoy the meetings," Greg said.

"I love them," Lisa said. "They always make me feel great."

"I wish I could say that," I said. "Sometimes they make me feel better, but other times worse."

"You'll get better as time goes on. You're still detoxing," Greg said.

"How long does it take to detox?" I said.

"It depends on the person, but at least a few months," Lisa said.

"No wonder I feel so uncomfortable," I said.

"Only the meetings and working with others will help that feeling," Greg said.

"What if I feel like leaving in the middle of a meeting?" I said.

"Try to sit through it," Greg said. "It's important to sit through those feelings. Eventually the bad feelings will subside."

"I want to get where you are," I said to Greg and Lisa.

"You will," Lisa said.

They gave me a lot of hope. Most of the time, when I was

104

alone, I felt hopeless, but when I was talking to them, I felt better. I asked Julie if she wanted to meet me at my house, and she agreed. When I got to my place, the cat was crying, because she hadn't been fed. I cleaned up quickly. The place was neat enough when Julie arrived a few minutes later.

"Why don't we listen to music?" I said.

"Sure."

I put on some jazz and thought for a second how nice it would be to have a bottle of wine. I quickly put that thought out of my head and sat on the couch next to Julie.

"I want to say something to you," Julie said.

"Sounds serious. What is it?"

"I know you're still seeing Jennifer," she said.

"How do you know?"

"Don't deny it. I know."

"We're only friends," I said.

"Listen. It's all right. I know you're confused right now, and I'm willing to wait. I've thought about it," she said.

"What do you mean by wait?" I said.

"I'm not going to have sex with you until you make up your mind," she said.

"I'm not having sex with Jennifer," I said.

"Don't lie to me," she said.

"What, are you spying on me now?"

"No. I know men well enough to know that if they're spending time with a woman, they're fucking her," she said.

"Jennifer and I are having serious problems. We've only fucked a couple of times in the last month," I said.

"That's why I'm willing to wait," Julie said.

I felt like I was being pressured into a decision. My respect for Julie increased immediately, and I felt like picking her right

105

then. I knew that no matter what I said, she wouldn't take me at my word.

"You're right, Julie. I'm glad you're willing to stick by me," I said.

"I like you. I should have never jumped right into bed with you," she said.

"No. We should have waited. I can't help myself sometimes," I said.

"I have a problem with it, too," she said.

"Let's start over," I said. "We'll go to meetings together, go out for dinner, go to the movies, everything but sex!"

"We can try, I guess."

"Sure. It'll be great," I said.

We sat quietly for a while, listening to the music. This would have been the time we would have made love, and there was a noticeable void. We were sitting very close to each other, and I was getting horny. I tried to kiss her, but she pushed me away.

"Can't we at least kiss?" I said.

"No, you know where that will lead," she said.

"We won't go any further. I promise," I said.

"Okay, maybe a little kiss," she said.

We kissed, and I gently pushed my tongue against hers. I put my arms around her and kissed her more passionately. After kissing for a few minutes, I put my hand on her breast—still no resistance. I slipped my hand under her shirt and bra and grabbed her naked breast.

"All right, that's enough," she said.

"Oh, come on. What are we, still in junior high?" I said.

"That's all you want me for!" she said.

"It is not. I love you," I said.

"Some love. I don't trust you."

"Why don't you trust me?" I said.

"Because you're sleeping with another woman!"

"I love you. I don't love her."

"I don't believe you. You're using both of us."

I didn't have an answer for her this time. I didn't feel like I was using either of them, but it certainly looked like it. The truth was that I was in love with both of them.

"Listen, Julie, I'm fine with not having sex with you right now, but you've got to believe me, I love you."

"I know you have strong feelings for me. We can talk about anything, but that's not love," she said.

"What is love then, if not strong feelings for each other?" I said.

"You have to build trust and respect," she said.

"I agree with that," I said.

"Well, as long as you're dating two of us, I can't trust you," she said.

"All right, I'll leave her," I said.

"Think about it. Don't say what's convenient. I'm going to go. I'll see you at the meeting tonight," she said.

Chapter 9

I was upset. It was at times like this that I felt like smoking pot. As the anger built, so did the cravings. I called my old pot dealer and told him I would be over in twenty minutes. I rationalized to myself that this would be the only time I got high, and that I would get back on the road to recovery the next day. I didn't call Greg like I should have. I was determined to get high. When I got to my dealer's house, I hardly spoke a word and bought a small bag of weed. I couldn't get my argument with Julie out of my mind. I went home and closed all the blinds. I made a makeshift pipe out of aluminum foil and filled the bowl. Suddenly, the anger shifted away from Julie toward myself. I was pissed off that I was so weak. I flushed the pot down the toilet and called Greg.

"Hey, what's up?" he said.

"I had a close call," I said.

"What happened?"

"I had an argument with Julie and went out and bought a bag of pot. But I flushed it down the toilet," I said.

"Why didn't you call me first?" he said.

"I knew you'd talk me out of it, and I thought I really wanted to get high," I said.

"You've got to do better than that," he said.

"I know. I hit a weak moment," I said.

"Meet me at the hall in half an hour," he said.

"All right."

I took a two-minute shower and put on some fresh clothes. I

108

was pissed at myself still and figured Greg would lecture me again, which I needed. I drove to the hall and waited a few minutes for Greg. There were some people hanging out, but I didn't really know any of them. Greg drove up with Lisa. I was glad to see her. I thought she might provide a buffer zone.

"Hey," I said.

"Hi," they said at the same time.

"I'm not going to do that again. I was freaking out," I said.

"You've got to do a better job of managing your life," he said.

"I know," I said.

"You say that, but you're reluctant to make any changes," he said.

"Don't give him a hard time," Lisa said. "He's still new."

"No. It's all right. I can take it," I said.

"That's all I'm going to say," he said.

"Thanks, bro. I'm glad you're there for me," I said.

"He means well," Lisa said to me.

Julie pulled up and waved to us from the car. She was wearing jeans and a shirt that came up above her navel. Her blonde hair was pulled back, and she was wearing a little makeup. She looked great.

"What's up, gang?" she said.

"Greg was telling me I have to do a better job of managing my life," I said.

"He's right," she said.

"I suppose you have yours down to a science," I said.

"No. I have to do better, too," she said.

"I'm sorry. I didn't mean that," I said.

"That's all right," Julie said.

"I have to stop seeing Jennifer. That's all there is to it," I said.

"I'm not saying a word," Greg said.

"He's full of shit, isn't he?" Julie said.

I was feeling very uncomfortable and decided to go home.

"I'm going to take off. I'll see you guys later," I said, and left.

Julie said not to leave, but I was pissed off. I immediately thought about getting some pot but didn't. I went home, turned on the TV, and sulked. I called my father and talked to him for a while. He made me feel better. I was so used to getting high to make myself feel good, that I couldn't stand being angry and sober. I fell asleep watching television and had strange dreams. I went to bed after getting up from the couch and had a lot of trouble falling asleep. I kept thinking about Julie, Jennifer, and Greg. Finally, I got up and called Julie.

"I'm sorry," she said. "I had no right to say anything."

"It's not your fault. I am full of shit," I said.

"I told you that I'm willing to stick by you," she said.

"I'm grateful for that. I don't know how long it's going to take for me to get straightened out, but I'm trying," I said.

"We're both going through the same thing," she said. "I've got a lot of problems, too."

"I'll call you in the morning," I said.

"Good night, sweetheart," she said.

I went to bed and tossed and turned again for what must have been two hours. Finally, I fell asleep and went back to the same dreamscape I was in before. It was a frightening landscape of strange men and women who were after me for some reason. I woke up and felt sorry for myself. I wanted to get high to ease the pain, but I fought it off. I took a hot bath and went back to bed. I fell asleep and didn't wake until morning. I was used to getting up early, and I felt tired from not enough sleep. I took a shower and dragged my ass to the meeting. Greg and Julie were already there.

"Hi, guys," I said.

"You look exhausted," Julie said.

"I didn't get enough sleep."

"You've got to get your sleep. It's so important," Greg said. "Maybe you should take a nap this afternoon."

"I will."

"I smoke more when I don't get enough sleep," Julie said.

"So do I," I said. "How's Lisa doing?"

"She's fine, but she really doesn't like her job," Greg said.

"I need to bring up a topic at this meeting," I said.

"What would that be?" Julie said.

"Unmanageability," I said.

"That would be good for me, too," she said.

We talked for a while, and I noticed that Julie was looking at me often. I wondered what she was thinking. I also thought that maybe I was losing my mind. We went into the meeting, and I brought up my topic. Everybody talked about the unmanageability of early recovery, and how important it was to fill your time with positive habits. I thought about it and realized I didn't have any habits. Now this was something I could work on. After the meeting, we went outside and smoked. It was cloudy out, but pretty warm.

"What did you work on when you first got sober?" I asked Greg.

"The only thing I could do, the last time, was not drink and get to as many meetings as I could," he said.

"I think I'm going to try going to bed and getting up at the same time every day," I said.

"I could do that, too," Julie said.

"That's a very good idea," Greg said, "and you should eat three meals a day, maybe get a job…"

"One thing at a time there, cowboy," I said, "but I would like to go back to work soon."

"How's the writing and painting going?" Julie said.

"They're really not going at all," I said, "except a little writing."

"Some alcoholics freeze when they get sober. They can't even function like they did when they were drunk," Greg said.

"I feel pretty frozen, but I'm doing a lot of thinking that eventually will translate into writing," I said.

"Some people, on the other hand, do twice as much to make up for lost time," Greg said.

"I want to be in the middle," I said. "I used to be a workaholic and ended up having a nervous breakdown."

"Easy does it," Julie said. "Do you want to come over for lunch?" she asked me.

"I'm going home to get some rest," I said.

I drove home and crashed. I couldn't sleep, but I closed my eyes and repeated the word "relax." I was in some kind of a trance and had pieces of dreams. I felt better when I got up. I made a sandwich and called my mother.

"Hi," she said, cheerfully.

"Hi, Mom."

"How did you sleep last night? You sound tired," she said.

"Not very well. I took a nap. I feel better."

"How's it going otherwise?"

"The cravings are pretty intense sometimes, but I'm getting through it," I said.

"Hang in there, honey. You'll be all right," she said.

After I hung up, I went back to bed. I fell into a deep sleep and dreamed that Jennifer was chasing me around the kitchen with a knife. I woke up startled and chuckled to myself. I realized that my dreams were bizarre, but I figured everybody's were. I decided to call Greg to see if he was going to an afternoon meeting. He said he was, so I got dressed and went out. When I got to the hall, Gregory was standing outside with Lisa.

"What are you doing here at this hour?" I said to Lisa.

"I just quit my job," she said.

"Without having another one first?" I said.

"Yup," was all she said.

"Well, I'm sure you can get another one pretty quickly," I said.

"There's a lot of demand for nurses," Greg said.

"I'm not worried about it," Lisa said. "Hey, here comes Julie."

Julie pulled up, but her car didn't sound too good.

"Sounds like you have a transmission problem," Greg said to Julie.

"Yeah, and I don't have the money to fix it."

"I'll help you," I said.

"It might be expensive," Greg said.

"We'll see," I said.

"Oh, thank you, Paul. You're such a good friend!"

I was thinking, of course, that this might persuade her to start sleeping with me again. I was not above ulterior motives. We went into the meeting, and Julie brought up the topic of frustration. Everybody had something good to say, except a couple of people, and I spoke of my frustrations, including fear of going back to work and managing my life better. I felt good this time, sharing, because I was more in touch with my real feelings. Outside again, we talked and smoked.

"I liked the way you shared today," Greg said to me.

"Yeah, it felt better, too."

"I didn't have a lot to say, except I'm frustrated with my work situation," Lisa said.

"It all helped me," Julie said.

"I'm going to take off this weekend," I said. "I need to get away."

"Can I go?" Julie said.

"Sure."

"Where do you want to go?" Julie said.

"Saratoga. I know some people there. I spent a few summers hanging out there," I said.

"Can we go tomorrow? I would love to go," Julie said.

"Okay. I'll call some hotels and see if I can make reservations."

"Oh, now I'm so excited," Julie said. "I'm going to go home and pack."

We left, and I went home to make some phone calls. I found a good hotel that wasn't too expensive, and I made reservations for two nights. I called Julie and asked her if she wanted to spend the night with me, so we could leave early in the morning. She agreed and came over.

"I probably packed too much, but it's better than not having enough," she said, as she put her two suitcases in my car.

"I'm only taking this bag," I said. "Come on in. I made us a salad."

We ate and then sat in front of the television.

"Tell me all about Saratoga. I've never even driven through it," Julie said.

"Well, there are lots of restaurants and cafés with tables outside, and everybody walks up and down the main streets," I said.

"Sounds so European," she said.

"Have you been to Europe?" I said.

"No, but I've seen pictures."

"Maybe I'll take you sometime."

"Now that would be some trip," she said.

"We'll go to Rome, Florence, and Paris."

"Don't promise something you can't come through with," she said.

"I'm not promising, only dreaming."

"It's been a dream of mine for a long time," she said.

It was at that point that I tried to kiss her. She pulled away. Apparently, she thought it was bad timing.

"I simply want to kiss you," I said.

"That's what you said the last time," she said.

"I'm serious this time. Let's make out a little," I said.

She gave me a dirty look and puckered her lips.

"Don't make fun of me," I said.

"Oh, stop being a little baby."

"What are we going to do in Saratoga? Sleep in different beds?" I said.

"Of course. What did you think?"

"I thought we'd be together," I said.

"Is that why you're taking me on this trip? So you can fuck me?" she said.

"No, that's not the sole purpose."

"But it is your main intention," she said.

"I wasn't even planning on taking you," I said.

"Well, if I go, we're not sleeping together, not until you drop Jennifer."

"I'm going to drop Jennifer. Don't worry about it," I said.

"When?"

"Right now. I'm going to call her in front of you and get it over with."

I dialed Jennifer's number, and several rings later, she picked up.

"Hi, Jennifer, it's me."

"I was hoping you'd call," she said.

"Listen, I have to tell you something."

"Sounds serious."

"It is. I can't see you anymore," I said.

"That's fine with me," she said, and hung up.

"I did it," I said to Julie.

"Great! Now things will settle down for you," she said.

I felt like I had cut off one of my fingers. I didn't enjoy breaking up with Jennifer. She had been through a lot with me. Now I was committed more to Julie, and I didn't like that either.

"Now will you sleep with me?" I said.

"Yes."

I grabbed her and pushed her down on the couch. We tore each other's clothes off and fucked our brains out.

"I was probably going to fuck you anyway," she said.

"Then I'll call Jennifer back up and see if she wants to go out with me again."

"Very funny. Hey, do you want to go to a meeting? Then we'll get up early and take off," she said.

"Sure. Let's go."

We drove to the hall. It must have been around eight thirty, and we found Greg outside, smoking.

"What's up, bro? You'll be very proud of me. I broke up with Jennifer. Now I only have one girlfriend."

"That should make your life a lot easier. How did she take

it?" Greg said.

"That's the funny thing about it. She didn't seem to care," I said.

"Even better," he said.

"I still don't trust him," Julie said.

"One has to build up trust over time," Greg said.

"And I plan on doing that," I said.

"We'll see," Julie said.

We went inside and were joined by Lisa a few minutes later. There weren't too many people at the meeting, which I liked, and it went pretty smoothly. I talked about trying to make my life more manageable and keeping my mood swings to a minimum. Julie talked about building trust and trying to become more confident. Afterwards, the four of us decided to go to the local coffee shop.

"I'm having decaf. I get all wound up during the meetings," Julie said.

"Me too. I want to make sure I get some sleep tonight," I said.

"Coffee puts me to sleep," Greg said.

"Yeah, then you wake up in the middle of the night and can't get back to sleep," Lisa said.

"That's not the coffee. I've always been that way," Greg said.

"I liked what you said about trust," Julie said to Greg.

"I had to learn how to trust myself and my higher power," Greg said. "I was out of control. My whole life was crazy. I had no good habits or instincts. My thoughts were all irrational. You have to put a little faith in a few other people to guide you."

"That's the problem for me," Julie said. "I don't know who to trust."

"You can trust me," Lisa said.

"I'm starting to feel that way," Julie said.

"I trust all of you," I said.

"Let it begin with small things and build up to larger things," Greg said.

"I think I trust too easily and then get burned," I said.

"But you're not trustworthy yet," Julie said.

"I'm trustworthy in some ways," I said. "You could give me fifty dollars, and I'd pay you back."

"That's not what I'm talking about," Julie said.

We talked for a while more. Then split up and went home. Julie came over to my house so we could leave early in the morning. We made love and went right to sleep. I had a nightmare about using cocaine and woke up in the middle of the night.

"What's the matter, honey?" Julie said.

"I had a terrible dream."

"Go back to sleep. Everything is fine," she said.

I couldn't go back to sleep and thought about all kinds of things. I kept Julie up as well and finally dozed off an hour or so later. I felt pretty good in the morning, and immediately made some coffee. Julie and I had a few cigarettes with the coffee and felt excited about our trip. I think Julie was glad to have me all to herself for a while.

"How long does it take to get there?" Julie said.

"About two and a half hours," I said.

"That's not long at all," she said.

"Did you mean what you said about me not being trustworthy?" I said.

"You play a lot of games. Let me put it that way," she said.

"We all play games," I said, "but if I say I'm going to do something, I usually do it."

118

"Usually is the operative word there," she said, laughing.

"Do you think you're trustworthy?" I said.

"Not always, I must admit," she said. "Why? Did I hurt your feelings? I didn't mean to."

"Yes, you hurt my feelings. Nobody likes to be called untrustworthy," I said.

"None of us were model citizens while we were drinking and using. It takes time to change. You know that," she said.

"I know, but I don't like my defects pointed out to me," I said. "Well, let's get going."

We decided to shower when we got there. We were anxious to get on the road. My car was all gassed up and ready to go. She didn't want to listen to my jazz, so she played with the radio all the way there. We didn't talk much. I was concentrating on the road. Traffic wasn't too heavy, and we arrived on time.

"I need to shower," Julie said. "Do you want to take one with me?"

"No, I'll nap for half an hour."

I tried to sleep but couldn't. I kept thinking about making love to Jennifer. Julie was a good sex partner, but Jennifer was better. I imagined her young, soft skin rubbing up against my body. I got a hard on thinking about it. Julie came out of the shower, and I attacked her. I fucked her hard.

"I love you," I said.

"You don't love me. You don't even know what love means," she said.

"Why do you have to say that? I know how I feel," I said.

"You don't know how you feel. You're only excited because we had sex. Love is a feeling that is developed over a long time," she said.

"We've been going out for a month or so. Doesn't that

qualify for love?" I said.

"No."

"Okay, have it your way. I don't love you," I said.

"I'm sorry. I shouldn't have been so harsh. I'm glad you feel close to me," she said.

"That's better," I said.

"Anyway, why don't you take a shower, and we'll go out for lunch," she said.

I took a hot shower and thought about how difficult life was in early recovery. I wanted to be in love but knew that I wasn't. I could feel waves of passion, intense passion, but then I would turn cold. I was up and down with all my feelings, and I had no rational control over them. After my shower, we walked out to the main street and walked along the boardwalk. There were beautiful shops and restaurants and lots of passersby. We stopped at a place that had a few free tables outside and sat in the warm breeze. I was feeling pretty good and let my thoughts wander wherever they wanted to.

"There's something I have to tell you," Julie said.

"What's that?"

"I have a daughter," she said.

"Really? Where is she? How old is she?"

"She's with her father in Montana, and she's seven years old."

"Why didn't you tell me before?" I said.

"I was afraid to. I didn't know what you'd think," she said.

"I think it's fine. I like kids," I said.

"I have a wicked resentment against her father. We had a long custody battle, and I lost," she said.

"Because you were drinking?"

"Yup."

"That's a shame," I said.

"I can see her for two weeks during the summer," she said.

"That's all? That's too bad," I said. "I'd like to meet her."

"You will."

We ordered some sandwiches, and I also got a cup of coffee. It was warm out, but the multicolored umbrellas shaded us. The breeze was nice, and it was interesting to watch the people walk by.

"Now that I'm sober, I'm going back to court," she said.

"You'll probably get joint custody. Are you sure you're ready for that?"

"I think I can handle it. A kid needs her mother," she said.

We ate and then strolled around the town for a while. We went back to the hotel and made love again. I was beginning to feel very strongly for her. The sex was getting more intense emotionally. I would spend a lot of time kissing her and caressing her before making love. I told her I loved her in the middle of sex. Afterwards, we showered together and took a long nap. I dreamed of being lost in a jungle and not being able to get out. I awakened with a start.

"What's wrong, sweetie?" Julie said.

"I had a bad dream."

"You have a lot of bad dreams, don't you?"

"It seems that way. I never remembered my dreams when I was smoking pot," I said.

"Your emotions are more intense now," she said. "I have some bad dreams, too."

"What do you dream about?" I said.

"I dream about my daughter getting in a car accident."

"The same dream over and over again?" I said.

"That's not the only one, but most of my bad dreams are

about my daughter," she said. "Let's go out again."

It was getting dark out, and the shops all had lights outside. The town was lit up, and there were still plenty of people walking around. It felt like a honeymoon to me, and I felt more at ease than I had in a long time. Julie seemed happy too. She had a glow about her. We went into a small bistro where they had only three items on the menu. It was still early and not crowded, but I could tell it was a popular spot. We sat by a window and ordered coffee.

"What's your daughter's name?" I said.

"Christine," she said.

"That's one of my favorite names," I said.

"Do you want to have kids?" Julie asked.

"Maybe, if I find the right woman," I said.

"I would like to have another child," she said.

"That's interesting," I said.

"Maybe we could have one," she said.

"I'll think about it," I said.

"Don't you think about it too long."

"You have a few good years of baby making ahead of you," I said.

"I don't want to be too old. There are three good years left."

"I'll keep that in mind," I said.

"I'm not putting any pressure on you. One child is enough, if that's what God wants," she said.

"I feel pressured though," I said.

The food came, and we ate in silence. I was thinking about whether I really wanted a child or not. The more I thought about it, the less it appealed to me. I liked children but taking care of one all the time seemed a real burden. I liked my freedom, and I liked my work. I didn't think I had time to raise a child. Now that Julie had told me she already had a child, I was put out.

"Well, I had to bring it up sooner or later," she said.

"I don't know about this," I said.

"I knew this would cause a problem. You can't make any kind of commitment," she said.

"I'm not ready to right now. That's for sure," I said.

"You're right. I sprung it on you, but there was no other way of telling you. At least I'm not pregnant," she said.

"Thank God for that," I said.

We finished eating, and I paid the bill. I was getting tired, and I felt like going to bed. We walked some more. The shops were dazzling, and I felt somewhat uneasy.

"Let's go back to the hotel," I said.

"Are you mad at me?" she said.

"I don't know. I think I need a meeting. Let's call the hotline and find out where there's a meeting tonight," I said.

"We went back to the hotel, and I immediately called the hotline. There was a meeting in a church nearby, so we walked down there about half an hour later.

"You're not speaking to me. I can tell you're mad," she said.

"I'm not mad."

"What's the matter then?"

"I'm thinking about my future," I said, "and it scares me."

"You've got such a bright future ahead of you. What could possibly scare you?"

"I don't make the best decisions."

"That'll change as you mature," she said. "I don't make such great decisions either."

"I have a big dream, and I don't feel like I'm getting any closer," I said.

"Now that you're sober, you can do anything you want to," she said.

"I love you," I said.

"That sounded more sincere than the last time. I love you, too," she said, smiling.

We entered the church and found the meeting in the basement. There were about a dozen people, and we still had a few minutes before the meeting began. I got some coffee and thought about a topic I would bring up. I had an uneasy feeling that needed to be quelled. When they asked for a topic, I raised my hand and said:

"Projecting negatively into the future."

They all nodded their heads, and it was very interesting to hear what they had to share. One woman talked about staying in the day, and in the now. She said when she had a lot of time on her hands, she would look deeply into her past and future, and be miserable by not enjoying the present moment. Another person said that we can't really know what's going to happen in the future, so there's no use worrying about it. Needless to say, I felt much better after the meeting. Julie and I walked outside and smoked.

"It's so interesting to hear people talk about the present moment," I said.

"What's so difficult for you in enjoying the present?" Julie said.

"I don't know. I'm always off in outer space," I said.

"You can still enjoy your thoughts, wherever they might go," she said.

"I do enjoy my ideas," I said.

"I don't think you worry too much about the future either," she said.

"No, I don't worry much, but I need these meetings to stay centered," I said.

We walked back to the hotel, and I felt again like we were on our honeymoon. I saw a cat scurrying into an alley and thought about my cat that I had left with my neighbor. My cat was so cool. She could simply chill out all day. When we got back to the room, I immediately thought about having sex. I grabbed Julie and threw her on the bed.

"What are you doing?" she said.

"I'm attacking you."

"I don't feel like having sex. I'm exhausted," she said.

"Oh, come on. We'll get in the bathtub. I'll get you in the mood," I said.

"Okay. I'll take a bath with you."

I went into the bathroom and turned on the hot water. I was thinking about how to turn her on and was already getting a hard on. When I came out, she was already naked, wearing her bathrobe.

"Why don't you do a striptease for me?" I said.

"You're perverted!"

"Am not," I said.

"Are too," she said, laughing.

She began to dance a little and flash parts of her body from under the robe. She started laughing uncontrollably and fell back on the bed next to me.

"Let's take a bath," I said.

We got in the bathtub with her in front. I soaped her back and her breasts, and she said she could feel my erection. I reached down, between her legs, and massaged her clit. She started moaning and leaning back against me.

"Slide back," I said.

She lifted herself up and sat on my cock. I was hard as a rock. It seemed impossible to make love in that position, so we go out and went to the bed after drying off. I licked her for a minute, then I climbed on top of her. I fucked her slowly for a while, then sped up.

"Did you come?" I said.

"No."

"Why not?" I said.

"Because you always try to please yourself and never worry about me," she said.

"That's not true," I said.

"You only licked me for a minute. You know that's the only way I can come," she said.

"I thought you could come when I'm inside you, too," I said.

"Only when I'm really excited," she said.

"I'm sorry. Next time I'll make you come. I promise," I said.

"It's all right. It felt good anyway," she said.

We went to sleep, and I slept well for the first time in a long time. I only woke up once all night, and I got up to smoke a cigarette. I was thinking, looking at Julie in the moonlight, that I was really lucky to have her. I went back to bed and fell right to sleep. In the morning, I got up before her and ordered some coffee from room service. Julie heard me moving around and got up.

"How did you sleep?" she said.

"Very well," I said. "How about you?"

"I had a very strange dream that my daughter was lost in the streets here," she said.

"Still dreaming about your daughter?" I said. "I wish I were a therapist. Maybe I could help you."

"I don't need therapy," she said.

"We all need therapy," I said.

The coffee came, and we lounged around in our pajamas for

126

an hour or so. It was raining that morning, and my mood went with the weather. I was feeling a little depressed, which was rare for me, and I didn't feel like going out, but Julie talked me into it. She wanted to go to a little café down the street for a pastry and a cappuccino.

"I don't yet feel comfortable being away from my house for two days," I said. "I like being at home."

"I like getting away," she said.

"I want to sleep in my own bed," I said. "Let's go back today."

"Oh, you're not serious, are you? We're having such a good time," she said.

"We'll stay the rest of the day and go back tonight. What do you say?" I said.

"Okay, if you insist," she said.

We walked to the café after showering, but we hadn't brought any umbrellas. We got a little wet but stayed mostly dry by walking along the edge of the buildings. I wanted to go to a meeting in the morning, but we went to the café instead. She ordered her pastry and cappuccino, and I got a latte. I was anxious to go home, but I didn't say another word about it. I couldn't shake my feeling of hopelessness, and there was no specific reason for my sadness.

"There are a few art galleries down that small side street I think we should go to," Julie said.

"That's fine with me," I said.

After our breakfast, we walked along the street that had several art galleries. Some of the work was interesting, and some was pretty bad, as is usual for most galleries.

"We should live here, and you could hang your work in these places," Julie said.

"I've often thought about living here," I said. "I used to really enjoy my summers here."

"Your paintings are better than most of the ones hanging in these galleries," she said.

"Thanks. I appreciate that," I said.

"You haven't painted since I've known you. Why is that?" she said.

"The pot used to motivate me. Now I simply don't have the desire," I said.

"Are you afraid to paint sober?" she said.

"A little, I guess," I said. "I don't know if I can produce the same quality."

"I'm sure you can. You have to get used to it," she said.

"I did do one, of a city scape, which is unusual for me, but it didn't turn out very well," I said.

"You're out of practice is all," she said. "It'll come back to you after a while."

"I hope so," I said.

We walked back to the hotel, and I noticed the rain had let up considerably. There were patches of blue sky, and it was a lot brighter out. It had warmed up a little, and it seemed like we were going to have a nice afternoon. I was still a bit depressed, so when we got back to the room, I called the hotline again and got a list of the meetings that day.

"There's a meeting in an hour at the same church if you want to go," I said.

"Sure, I'll go," she said.

We took a nap for a while, and I watched some stupid game show for half an hour while Julie read a magazine. I was thinking that maybe I was getting bored with her. I couldn't think of anything to talk about. I decided to call Gregory.

"Hey, what's up?" he said.

"Checking in, brother. What's up with you?"

"Lisa and I are sitting here watching the Nature channel, of all things. What are you doing?" he said.

"We're relaxing right now. We went out for breakfast, and now we're going to a meeting," I said.

"Good for you. That's a beautiful town," he said. "Hey, listen, I have an announcement to make. Lisa and I are getting married!"

"Married! Congratulations. When's the big day?" I said.

"We haven't decided yet. We're going to wait a year," he said.

Julie's face lit up as she heard me talking.

"How are you feeling, by the way? This is your first time away from home," Greg said.

"I'm somewhat restless and depressed, I must admit," I said. "We're coming home tonight."

"Did you enjoy yourself a little anyway?" he said.

"Yeah, it was nice to see the town again. I miss it," I said.

"Maybe you can make the late meeting tonight," he said.

"Sure. We'll see you there," I said.

After I got off the phone, I told Julie that they were going to wait a year before they got married.

"Perhaps we can have a double ceremony," Julie said.

"I don't know about that," I said.

"You're so afraid of commitment. You told me you loved me," she said.

"We've only been going out for a few weeks, and now you're already talking about marriage," I said.

"I think we'd be good together. I enjoy your company, and the sex is good," she said.

"I think we'd be good together, too, but I want to wait a while first," I said.

"A year is a long time," she said.

"I was thinking more like two or three," I said.

"We'll be broken up by then," she said.

"Then it'll be a good thing we're not married," I said.

"Let's go to the meeting," she said.

When we arrived at the church, there were a few people outside smoking. We introduced ourselves to another couple and chatted about how Saratoga had changed. The meeting started and Julie brought up the topic of fear. I laughed to myself, but I thought it would be a good topic. One man said that one had to feel the fear and walk right through it. Another woman said that she had had a lot of fears in early recovery, but that most of them had evaporated on their own. At the end of the meeting, Julie said that some of her fears were subsiding, but that many of them were irrational and popping up out of nowhere.

Afterwards, as we were walking back to the hotel, I thought about my fear of being away from home.

"Why do you think I feel so uncomfortable on this trip?" I said.

"I don't know. It's one of those irrational fears. You're not used to it sober," Julie said.

"I think when you stay in one environment for a long time, it feels strange to move into another one," I said.

"I'm sure that's part of it," she said, "and also when you're newly sober, everything feels strange."

I looked into this shop that had pastries on display, and Julie and I decided to go in. It reminded me of Europe, and we bought a few pastries to take with us.

"I wonder how long it'll take me before I take another trip to

Italy," I said.

"It might be a while," she said.

"It's ironic because I want to get away so badly, and then when I arrive, I want to go right back," I said.

"You'll settle down after a while. I feel the same way to a degree. What time are we leaving?" she said.

"I think we should pack up and go," I said.

"Okay."

We got to the hotel a few minutes later, and I went to the front desk to check out. We went upstairs, and I asked her if she wanted to have sex before we left. She said no. I laughed at the way she said it, and she laughed, too. It only took us a few minutes to pack, and we left shortly thereafter. On the way home, we spent some time pointing out beautiful trees and houses that we passed. It was a very pleasant ride, and our conversation was light. Two hours later, we arrived at my home and took a little nap. I wanted to have sex, but she didn't want to.

"You always want to have sex, don't you?" Julie said.

"I'm a normal male in that respect, I think, once or twice a day," I said.

"Well, three times a week is good for me," she said.

"We've been doing it a lot more than that," I said.

"I know, but I'm talking about after it becomes routine, and we're together a long time," she said.

"Can't we wait until we cool off naturally?" I said.

"I guess so, but you're always asking me. It's annoying," she said.

"I'm sorry. I didn't know it bothered you," I said.

After we slept for a while, Julie went home. I was glad to be alone for a bit. It was difficult for me to be around somebody for a long period of time. I took a hot bath and reflected about the trip to Saratoga. I felt more and more comfortable with Julie, and I was thinking that maybe I should marry her. She had opened up to me, and we were beginning to get into a nice routine. We had decided to go to the meeting that night, so I dressed and called my mother.

"Hi, honey," she said.

"I went to Saratoga for two days with Julie. It was great," I said.

"How nice! Did you see Charlie?"

"No, I didn't call him. I'm going to wait a while before I get in touch with him," I said.

"How do you feel today?" she asked.

"I'm feeling pretty good. I think I'm beginning to stabilize. My mood swings are less intense and less frequent," I said.

After talking to my mother for a while, I went to the night meeting. Gregory, Lisa, and Julie were already there. We smoked for a while and joked around. It was so nice to laugh without being high. Julie was making me laugh for a change, which really felt good. Gregory was always funny.

"Paul wanted to have sex twelve times a day!" Julie said.

"What's wrong with that?" Gregory said. "You should give him credit for his stamina. I can only do it eight or nine times."

"You never want to do it!" Lisa said. "Except in the morning, before I've had my coffee."

"That's the problem," Gregory said. "You're a night person, and I'm a morning person. I think we have to compromise and do it about two in the afternoon."

"I could do that," Lisa said.

"No, I forgot, that's when I'm taking my nap," Greg said, laughing.

"Paul's good at taking naps, too," Julie said.

"That's because I'm so tired from having sex," I said.

The meeting started, so we filed in after everybody else. Lisa wanted to bring up a topic, but she waited too long, and a woman beat her to it. She brought up the topic of resentments. She was going through a divorce and custody battle, and I couldn't help but think of Julie's situation. The woman was in tears as she told her tale of woe. When it came to Julie's turn, I was surprised that she passed. I thought maybe she didn't want to break down. I said that she had to take care of herself first and leave it to fate to see how it played out. Gregory said that her feelings of depression would pass, and that she had to think of the children first. After the meeting, we went outside to smoke, as usual.

"How are you doing?" I said to Julie.

"I'm all right, I guess," she said.

"You're a good woman, Charlie Brown," Lisa said.

"It's all so difficult," Julie said, with tears in her eyes.

"It'll get better," Gregory said.

"When?" she said.

"Soon enough. You're going to have to be patient," Greg said.

"I don't get to see my daughter, and he's taking advantage of me," Julie said.

"The longer you stay sober, the more things straighten out," I said. "Do you want to come home with me?"

"Yes, I think so."

Julie and I drove to my house, and she was feeling a little better by the time we arrived. It was a warm evening out, and the stars were shining. I looked up at the stars and wondered why life had to be so complicated. There were no answers in the sky, only more mysteries. Julie walked inside first, and I followed, noticing how she walked with her head bent down. I felt so sorry for her but didn't know what to say. There was tension between us, for no apparent reason, and I didn't know how to get rid of it.

"Do you want to take a hot bath?" I asked her.

"Okay, but no sex," she said.

"No, I wasn't thinking about that," I said.

We took a nice hot bath together, and I rubbed her back with some soap. It was very soothing as we listened to the jazz emanating from the other room. We didn't talk much, and the hot water proved to be very therapeutic. I thought about her problems mostly and was not too worried about my own. I couldn't help but to look deeply into the future and imagine us married with children, having a normal life. We went to bed, and I couldn't sleep because Julie kept tossing and turning. Finally, we both fell asleep. I had a few dreams, but the only one I could remember was about Julie and her daughter. It ended with them saying goodbye to me and fading into the distance. I woke up to find Julie already out of bed.

"Hello?" I said, checking to see if she was still in the apartment.

"I'm here," she said from the kitchen.

"Is there any coffee?" I said.

"It's all ready," she said.

"I'll be right there."

I was a little tired but felt good. The coffee tasted great, and I was relieved to see that Julie was in a good mood.

"Do you want some eggs?" she asked.

"No, this is fine."

"I sleep better when I'm with you," she said.

"Same here," I said.

"I don't dream as much either," she said.

"That's interesting," I said. "You didn't have any bad dreams last night, did you?"

"No, not one," she said.

"That's great. Things are starting to turn around for you," I said.

"I don't know about that," she said, "but I feel good today at least."

"Keep a positive attitude," I said.

"I'll try. Do you want to go to the meeting this morning?"

"I think I'm going to do a painting," I said.

"Okay. That'll give me a chance to clean up around here," she said.

I organized myself and painted for an hour, which felt great since I hadn't done it in a while. I did a seascape, with blues and greens, and a small house next to the water. It looked like a stormy day on the ocean, and I was pleased with the way it turned out. Every once in a while, Julie would come into my studio to see how I was doing.

"That turned out great!" she said.

"Thanks, honey. I liked it, too."

"See, you're not so out of practice," she said.

"I guess I can do this sober," I said.

"Of course you can. Remember, feel the fear and walk right through it."

"Easier said than done," I said, "but I'm pleased with this."

"Your writing will come along, too. You'll see," she said.

"I'm glad you're so supportive," I said.

We decided to take a nap, and she was in the mood for sex, so we fucked for a while, and I came inside her without any protection.

"Do you think that was a good idea?" she said.

"I couldn't help myself," I said.

"I understand, but now I'm going to have to get a pill."

"I'll go with you," I said.

After we went to Planned Parenthood, we went to a meeting. It was early afternoon. The clouds shaded the sun, and it felt cool. Gregory was there, hanging out with a few of his friends, and he waved to us as we pulled in.

"Did you come inside me on purpose?" Julie said.

"No. I told you I couldn't help myself."

"I think you were trying to make me pregnant," she said.

"Not until we're married," I said.

"Then you're thinking that we're going to get married," she said, "and that then we're going to have children?"

"You take me too literally," I said.

"How am I supposed to take you, Professor?" she said.

"I wasn't trying to make you pregnant," I said.

"Okay, I believe you," she said.

We got out of the car and walked over to Greg.

"Hey, how are you?" he said.

"Fair to middling," I said.

"Hanging in there?" he said.

"Sure," Julie said.

"I have some mood swings, still," I said. "The slightest negative comment makes me feel like shit."

"Have you been giving him a hard time?" Greg said to Julie.

"Not really. I think I've been very nice," she said.

"She has been. I don't take things well, I guess," I said.

"It'll get better," Greg said.

We walked into the meeting, and there was a guy there who was obviously drunk and smoking a cigar. I didn't think it was too funny, but Greg chuckled. The meeting began, and I was surprised that nobody kicked this man out. Suddenly, the man started raving and ranting, and somebody escorted him out. I didn't know why, but I was shaken up.

"Don't worry about it," Greg said to us. "It happens every once in a while."

"I never acted like that!" I said.

"I'm sure you had your moments. He's a very sick man," Gregory said.

We sat through the meeting, but I couldn't concentrate on anything that was said. Julie seemed all right, and she even shared a bit. Afterwards, we went out and smoked.

"This disease is wicked," I said.

"He does this every few months. He lives on the street, and nobody can seem to help him. People give him money, which he spends on booze. It's awful," Greg said.

"I heard that only three percent ever recover from alcoholism," Julie said.

"It's true," Greg said.

"Wow! That's some statistic," I said.

"The common view is though, that most alcoholics live on the street and don't function. Nothing could be further from the truth," Greg said.

"I don't ever want to go back to that hell," Julie said.

"It wasn't always hell for me. I must admit we had some good times, but it got out of hand," I said.

"Mine was hell," Gregory said.

"But your life is so much better now," Julie said to Greg.

"How do you keep from dwelling on the past is what I want to know?" I asked Greg.

"As you stay sober longer, you establish a sober past, and the distant past fades away for the most part," he said.

"The echoes are so strong now," I said.

"It's going to take some time," he said.

"My nightmare hasn't even ended yet," Julie said. "It's going on and on."

"As you straighten things out, you'll begin to feel better," Greg said. "I'm living testimony. My life was far worse than yours, and now it's pretty good, but I had to work hard to improve it."

"What kind of work can make you, or allow you, to forget the past?" I said.

"Writing it down and telling it to another person," Greg said, "and therapy."

"But therapy stirs up everything, and makes it boil over. You have to remember," I said.

"Yes, but you deal with it, like in dreams," he said. "Remembering allows you to forget."

"That's interesting," I said.

"I wish I could forget everything," Julie said.

We decided to leave, and Julie said she would come over to my house. For some reason, I was filled with optimism. Listening to Gregory had lessened my burden, and I was looking forward to a day that I wouldn't be haunted by my past. It wasn't that I thought about my past all the time, but every so often, something would trigger a painful memory, and I would run with it until I was exhausted with pain. I didn't have any resentment toward people, only painful actions that I had done. Julie wanted to eat something, so we ordered pizza.

"Are you afraid of going to sleep sometimes?" Julie asked me.

"Not really, I don't think," I said. "Why? Are you?"

"Sometimes I feel scared," she said.

"Afraid of what, specifically?" I said.

"I don't know if I'm afraid of never waking up again, or simply worried about everything, but I feel this fear," she said.

"It'll probably go away eventually," I said. "It may be a symptom of early recovery."

"Why does everything have to be a symptom of early recovery?" she said.

"Are you angry now?" I said. "Your anger may stem from your fear."

She was silent for a while, and I sensed she was angry at herself, and not me. There was really no reason for her to be angry at me, but moods can be transferred slightly, and I felt sad. I didn't like to see her upset, and I felt I couldn't help her.

"I wish I could escape," she said.

"I wish I could, too," I said, "but how without getting into the drugs again?"

"Maybe meditation," she said. "We haven't tried that."

"That's a good idea," I said. "I learned a technique in college."

I went into the kitchen to get a candle and put it on the floor in front of us. I explained the technique to Julie, and we sat there for twenty minutes, staring at the candle and clearing our minds. It worked beautifully.

"That was great!" Julie said.

"I know. I'm surprised. I haven't tried it in a long time," I said.

"I feel so calm and relaxed," she said.

"Let's try to do that in the morning," I said, "before the meeting."

"I'm going to bed early tonight," I said.

I went to bed and fell right to sleep.

Chapter 10

I don't know if it was the meditation or a clear mind, but I slept right through the night and didn't feel Julie next to me at all. I woke up feeling better than I had in years and hopped right out of bed. Julie was already in the kitchen. The coffee was ready, and she was making eggs.

"I slept so well last night," I said.

"So did I."

"Let's meditate again after breakfast," I said.

It felt nice to eat breakfast together under normal conditions. She had made scrambled eggs with toast, and everything was perfect. The kitchen smelled of coffee, and the sun was peeking through the window. After breakfast, we sat on the floor in the living room and meditated. I repeated a word in my mind and tried not to think about anything else. We stared at the candle for twenty minutes.

"That felt good. Now I can be relaxed for the whole day," she said.

I didn't tell Julie, but I thought about Jennifer while I was meditating. I had a picture of her naked in my mind and imagined licking her pussy. I almost felt guilty about it, but not really. I figured I hadn't done anything, so why feel guilty. Then it occurred to me that maybe I could call her up when Julie wasn't around. I quickly put that out of my mind.

"We should do this every morning," I said.

"We will, definitely," she said.

140

"Let's shower and go to the meeting," I said.

We showered together, and even though we didn't make love, we caressed each other, and it felt great. After we dressed, I drove us to the meeting, and we were pleasantly surprised to see Lisa with Gregory.

"Hey, what's up?" I said.

"Oh nothing. We're madly in love," Lisa said.

"So are we," Julie said, looking at me.

Julie and Lisa walked off to talk to each other, so Gregory and I talked, too.

"We meditated last night, and this morning it was great," I said.

"I meditate, too," he said.

"I must admit though, I had some thoughts about Jennifer while I had my eyes closed," I said with a laugh.

"Thoughts are okay, but don't act on them," he said. "Try to stay with Julie for a while. It'll calm your nerves."

"No, you're right, of course, but I'm starting to feel some pressure from her. I know she wants to marry me, but I'm not ready," I said.

"She shouldn't be talking about marriage at this stage. It's too soon," he said.

"I know. I'm not even on my feet yet. I can't settle down," I said.

"It's going to be a while before you feel comfortable in your own skin," he said.

"I feel comfortable while I'm meditating and for a little bit afterwards," I said.

"That's good, and I'm sure you feel pretty good after meetings, too," he said.

I reflected on my recent past and how I felt after doing

certain things. I always felt productive after writing or painting something. I was trying to go with the flow and not be too preoccupied. I enjoyed talking to Gregory, and I wished that I felt the same way about talking to Julie. The sun was out, and it was getting pretty warm, so Greg and I walked inside where it was cooler. I thought for a second how nice it would be to walk along the beach in California and wondered why I had given that up.

"Why can't I be satisfied with one woman?" I asked Gregory.

"You're not comfortable with yourself, that's why," he said. "I went through that, too, but now Lisa satisfies all my needs."

"I can't wait until I'm in that position. Do you think it'll happen for me, too?" I said.

"Sure, if you work at it," he said.

"I love Julie, but I'm still attracted to Jennifer. I'm not going to deny it," I said.

"Why don't you not date either of them, until you straighten things out in your mind?" he said.

"I don't know if I can do that," I said. "I'm worried I'll get too lonely."

"Then date both of them without sleeping with either of them," he said. "That way you can spend time with them and decide later."

"Maybe I could do that," I said, thinking that I couldn't give up the sex.

I looked outside the big picture window and saw the blue sky with a few clouds, and I thought that maybe I would have a bright future ahead. It was very calming to talk to Gregory. He was mature and understanding. He had been through a lot, so that now his life was relatively smooth. His eyes were calm and relaxed, which gave him a look of wisdom.

"Were you involved in a few love triangles?" I asked him.

"Sure, and it didn't feel good either," he said.

"How were they resolved?"

"I married one gal and left the other one, but a few times I ended up with neither of them," he said.

"What happened to your marriage?" I said.

"It ended because she got tired of my drinking too much," he said. "She was a wonderful woman, too. I fucked that up."

"Yeah, but now you're getting married again, and everything is fine," I said.

"That's true. Thank God for Lisa," he said.

The meeting began, and the girls came inside. I was glad to see that the drunken man hadn't shown up. It was a small crowd, and I was hoping that I got a chance to speak. Julie had a big smirk on her face; apparently she and Lisa had been laughing. I wanted Julie to make me laugh more, but I had to accept her the way she was. The topic of the meeting was loneliness, and I thought I might have a lot to say on the subject. When it came to my turn to speak, all I could say was that it was all right to be alone some of the time, but that it was important to spend time with other people. Loneliness is a state of mind that you can feel even when you're with somebody else.

Then Julie said: "I feel lonely all the time, even when I'm with Paul. I'm working on keeping my mind interested in things and people so that I don't feel that way."

I hadn't realized that Julie felt like that, and I wondered what I could do about it. After the meeting, we went outside into the bright sunshine.

"I didn't know you felt lonely all the time," I said to Julie.

"I think you shut me out of your emotional life," she said.

"I thought I was being open to you," I said.

"You don't tell me all your secrets," she said.

"I don't tell you everything I'm thinking, but I tell you the important things," I said.

"There's so much more about you that I want to know. I don't believe our conversations are profound enough," she said.

"We talk about everything. I can't help it if I'm not profound enough," I said.

"I don't mean profound, really, but intimate is what I'm trying to say," she said.

"I'll try to tell you my deepest feelings," I said.

Gregory and Lisa had left right after the meeting, and Julie and I decided to go back to my house. I was hungry, so we stopped at a sandwich shop and got something.

"Do you think I'm getting fat?" Julie said.

"Don't be ridiculous," I said.

"See how you lie to me?" she said.

"I don't lie to you. Let's not start an argument over such a trivial thing," I said.

"It's not trivial. I've gained five pounds since I've known you," she said.

"Well, I haven't noticed it," I said. "Besides everybody fluctuates five to ten pounds."

"I'm getting fat," she said.

"All right, you're getting fat," I said.

"See, now you're being honest," she said, laughing.

We got in the car, laughing, and drove to my house in a good mood. I was thinking that I wanted to fuck her but didn't know how she'd feel about it. When we got inside, I went immediately into the kitchen to make coffee. She turned on the music and sat on the couch. We were listening to Stan Getz, and he was putting me in the mood. I didn't know if I should start kissing her or

144

simply ask her if she wanted to have sex. I decided to kiss her on the cheek to see how she responded. When I tried to kiss her, she said: "I'm not in the mood."

"I wasn't thinking about sex," I said. "I only wanted to give you a loving kiss."

"Yeah, I know you. You want to have sex," she said.

"Can't we, please?"

"No."

"Why not?"

"I'm not in the mood."

"Will you be in the mood later?" I said.

"Maybe," she said.

"Good enough for me," I said.

We sat on the couch and listened to the jazz. It was getting later in the afternoon, and clouds had covered the sky. I was feeling like Julie and I were not communicating well, but I also thought there was no rational evidence for that feeling. I missed Jennifer. I could hear Gregory's voice in my head, and I started to be confused. When I was with Julie, I wanted to be with Jennifer, and vice versa. I wasn't bored exactly, but restless. I knew, too, that this was one of my particular symptoms of early sobriety.

"I think I need to be alone for a while," I said.

"That's fine. I'll take off. Call me later," she said.

"I will."

As soon as Julie left, I called Jennifer.

"Hello?" she said.

"Hi, sweetheart," I said.

"What do you want?" she said.

"I want to apologize," I said.

"What good do you think it will do?"

145

"I made a big mistake by breaking up with you," I said.

"Do you really think I'm going to take you back so easily?" she said.

"I was depressed when I talked to you. I wasn't in my right mind," I said.

"That's some excuse," she said.

"Do you miss me?" I said.

"I must admit I do, a little," she said.

"I miss you, too," I said.

I could tell by the tone of her voice that she was softening a bit. All I could think about was her naked body.

"Are you still going out with that other girl?" she said.

"No. We've decided to be friends only," I said.

"Are you lying?" she said.

"No, I swear," I said. "We don't have much in common, and she's thinking of going back to her husband."

"Why does everybody go back and forth to their old relationships? I want to move on," she said.

"Don't you want to go back out with me?" I said.

"I don't know. We'll see," she said.

I was thinking that eventually I could talk her into going back with me, but I wanted to take it slowly. I knew that she missed our conversations and that she was lonely. I felt a little guilty, but that wasn't going to stop me.

"How's school going?" I said.

"Pretty well, but I'm still having trouble with my theory course. Maybe you could help me," she said.

"I'd love to help you," I said.

"That doesn't mean we're going out again," she said.

"I know, I know," I said. "We'll think about that."

All I cared about was that she was interested in spending

time with me. I thought about Julie but put her out of my mind.

"I'll call you later. Maybe we can get together tomorrow," I said.

"Okay."

Suddenly, I was very happy. I had felt a loss before, and now I felt that I had got something back. I had no idea how I would handle the two of them again, but I was willing to try. I thought I wouldn't tell Gregory about it, but I knew that would be hard. He was the only person I was honest with. I decided to call Greg because I was beginning to feel uncomfortable.

"Hey, what's up?" he said.

"I'm fucking up again," I said.

"What did you do now?" he said, laughing.

"I called Jennifer and got back with her," I said.

"You're crazy," he said.

"I know I am. I can't help myself. When I am with one, I think about the other. Is that normal?" I said.

"Nobody knows what normal is. I guess as long as you're not using and drinking, you can do whatever you want," he said.

"I want to feel comfortable though, and I know I can't if I go on this way," I said.

"I can only give you advice. I can't make you take it," he said. "Things will straighten themselves out on their own," he said.

I wondered for a second which way fate would take me, but then realized that my destiny was up to my own decisions. I had to think this through and make a good decision. I was scared.

"Thanks bro. I'll probably see you later," I said.

Chapter 11

I stayed alone that evening and surprisingly didn't feel that lonely. I was able to do some writing, and I listened to jazz. I made some pasta for dinner and actually enjoyed cooking for myself. After dinner, I called Jennifer.

"What's up?" she said.

"I'm wondering what you've been thinking," I said.

"To tell you the truth, it hasn't been good," she said. "I think you're lying to me about the other woman."

"I'm not lying. We've decided to be friends. She's still in love with her husband," I said.

"We can spend time together, but I'm not going to sleep with you," she said.

"That's all right. I can wait," I said.

"Wait for what?" she said.

"Until you trust me again," I said.

"That might be a long time," she said.

"I love you, Jennifer."

"I love you, too, but I don't trust you," she said.

"We can work on that," I said. "I'll talk to you tomorrow."

"Okay."

When I got off the phone, I felt disheartened. I also felt like an ass. I decided to call Julie immediately.

"Hi," I said.

"I thought you wanted to be alone," she said.

"I've been alone enough tonight. I actually cooked for

myself."

"Good for you! I quit my job," she said.

"I noticed you hadn't been going in, but I thought you were just taking some time off," I said.

"My ex has decided to give me more money. I threatened to take him to court," she said.

"Are you going to go back to school?"

"That's my plan," she said.

"Great! I'll help you as much as possible," I said.

"I'm taking nursing, so you won't really be able to help," she said.

"I'll wash out the bed pans," I said.

"Do you want me to come over?" she asked.

"Yes, I really would."

After I hung up, I decided to clean a little before she came over. I made the bed and dusted the whole apartment. The place was never cluttered, but it was always dusty. Julie liked to clean for me. It made her feel needed. I put on some Stan Getz, and it occurred to me that it would have been the perfect time for champagne. When she arrived, the apartment had a nice atmosphere. I had a lot of paintings hanging on the walls, and some were lit from behind. I should have been living in the village in New York, but I couldn't afford it.

"Hi, honey," I said, giving her a kiss.

"I brought some chocolates," she said, smiling.

"I was thinking of getting some champagne, but I figured it wasn't appropriate," I said with a laugh.

"I wonder what it would have been like if we had known each other before sobriety?" she said.

"If you think it's difficult now, then it would have been impossible," I said.

"You wouldn't have tolerated my behavior. I was out of control," she said.

"I wasn't exactly out of control, but the last couple of years I wasn't doing much," I said.

"Sometimes I don't even know how I survived," she said. "I did so many dangerous things. I guess I got lucky."

"Don't forget where you came from," I said, "and I won't forget either."

We listened to the music for a while, and I began to think about having sex with her. I realized that my success depended on how I approached her. I couldn't be too forward, or she would be turned off. I decided to snuggle with her and see if she made the first move. I put my arm around her shoulders and rested my head against her. She kissed me on my forehead. I waited patiently for what seemed a long time and put my head in her lap. She leaned over and kissed me on the mouth.

"I love you," I said.

"I love you, too."

I put my hand on her breast and rubbed ever so gently. She closed her eyes and moaned. I turned my head into her and kissed her belly. She put her hand on my lap and massaged my cock.

"Let's go in the bedroom," I said.

"Okay."

We went into the bedroom, and I pushed her on the bed. She started to take her clothes off, but I stopped her.

"Not yet," I said.

I got on the bed with her and put my hands all over her body. Then, slowly, I unbuttoned her shirt. After I undressed her, I let her undress me. When we were naked, I got on top of her and started to insert myself. She stopped me.

"Why don't you want to lick me? You always enjoyed doing

that," she said.

"I don't know. I don't feel like doing it. That's all," I said.

"You don't like my body any more. I guess I don't compare to your young friend," she said.

"That's not it. I'm not in the mood for that. No big deal," I said.

"Then I don't want to do it," she said.

"But why?"

"That's the only way I can orgasm," she said.

"You can orgasm during intercourse," I said. "You have before."

"Not really. I faked it," she said.

"Faked it?"

"It still felt good, but I don't come that way," she said.

"Now you tell me," I said.

I got off her and put my clothes back on without saying another word. Now I was frustrated and angry and didn't know how to react. I felt like kicking her out but thought better of it. I wanted to say something hurtful but didn't. She got up and put her clothes on, but she didn't seem angry. I wanted to get high in the worst way, but I knew that wasn't the solution either.

"Do you want me to go?" she said.

"No. Don't go. I'll cool off in a minute," I said.

"Don't be mad at me. I only faked it to protect your feelings," she said.

"I know, but now I have this feeling that I can't satisfy you," I said.

"You're a good lover. You know that," she said. "I want you to go down on me sometimes."

"I don't mind doing that, but not all the time," I said. "You don't suck me very often."

151

"I guess you're right," she said.

I still wanted to make love to her, but the moment was gone. We went out to the living room and watched TV until it was time to go to sleep. She fell asleep right away, but it took me an hour before I dozed off. I woke up three hours later with a start. Slowly but surely, I remembered the dream I was having.

I dreamed that I was living with both Jennifer and Julie. There was something different about them, but I could still identify them. Julie was taking on the role of wife, while Jennifer was my daughter. I was in bed with Julie, waiting for her to fall asleep, when I snuck out and got into bed with Jennifer, who trusted me implicitly. I made love to Jennifer, kissed her on the forehead, and went back to bed with Julie. Julie woke up and started screaming at me while I denied everything. Then I woke up.

The dream didn't sit well with me. I tried going back to sleep but couldn't. I got up, trying not to disturb Julie, but she woke up.

"What's the matter?" she said.

"Bad dream," I said. "I'm going to make some coffee and watch TV."

I made the coffee and was glad to see Julie get up and join me.

"You don't have to get up," I said.

"I don't mind. You would do it for me," she said.

"I'm not sure I would," I said, laughing.

"Do you want me to make you something to eat, maybe some eggs?" she said.

"That would be nice," I said. "I'll make the bacon."

We cooked together in the middle of the night, and I felt a sense of peace. I looked out the window at the streetlight, and it reminded me of the nights I would stay up and hang out with my friends. I was glad I was on a new path, and no matter now unmanageable my life was, it was better than before. We ate in silence and decided to go back to bed right afterwards. It took me a while to get to sleep, but I didn't dream any more that night. Julie wasn't affected by the coffee and fell right to sleep. In the morning I felt tired but got out of bed fairly early. Julie was in the kitchen with coffee.

"Good morning, sweetheart," I said.

"How do you feel? You didn't sleep well last night," she said.

"I'm tired, but I feel all right," I said.

"Do you want to skip the meeting this morning?" she asked.

"No, I want to go," I said.

We had coffee and then showered together. We didn't have sex, but she massaged me with soap, and it felt great. The shower revived me, as did the coffee, and I felt pretty good. Julie put on a nice white dress. She had a few clothes at my place, and her legs looked sexy. I thought about Jennifer for a second, but I put her out of my mind.

"You know," I said to her as we got in the car, "all my bad dreams seem fear based, and they're like this long fiction that takes various twists and turns. They're very interesting, but I certainly don't know how to interpret them."

"Maybe the fact that they point out to you that you're afraid of something is enough," she said.

"But what am I afraid of?" I said.

"What was your dream last night?" she said.

"I've forgotten," I said.

"Next time, try to see what the fear is," she said. "Maybe that will give you a clue."

"I'll try," I said.

I thought about my dream the night before and realized that there was a Freudian flavor to it that disturbed me greatly. I had never seen Jennifer as my daughter in my conscious life, so there was another secret about it that I couldn't figure. We arrived at the hall a few minutes later, and I was pleased to see Gregory standing outside. There were a few people hanging out, some of whom I had met, and others whom I had not.

"Hey, what's up?" Gregory said as we approached.

"Weird night," I said.

"You'll get those once in a while," he said.

"We got up in the middle of the night, and Julie cooked breakfast," I said.

"How romantic," he said.

"I try," Julie said.

"I had another bad dream," I said.

"About drinking or using?" he said.

"I don't remember," I said. "All I know is that it was frightening."

"It's only a dream. You'll have those for a while, but they'll taper off," he said.

"I have some dreams about losing my daughter," Julie said, "but I know if I stay on track, I'll get her back."

"That's right. You two should stick together. You can keep each other sober," Greg said.

"I guess that's what we're doing," I said. "She definitely gives me more strength."

"You do, too, for me I mean," Julie said.

We went inside for the meeting and sat by the door so I could sneak out in the middle and have a cigarette. The topic was self-pity, and I could identify with a lot of the things that were said. I didn't have too much self-pity, but when I did, it seemed to build on me until I thought to myself that my life sucked. When it was Julie's turn to speak, she was very serious.

"A lot of times I feel sorry for myself because of the difficult position I put myself in. I don't blame other people any more, though. I've done that, too, but I blame myself, and I'm very hard on myself. I'm hoping that since I'm in recovery, I can dig myself out of the hole that I dug. Thank you," she said.

"I don't feel sorry for myself a lot, but when I'm in a bad mood, I tell myself all kinds of negative things. I'm trying to be more positive and look on all the gifts I have. Thank you," I said.

"I don't feel sorry for myself any more, but when I was incarcerated, I blamed the system and thought that I was a victim. Now I see that I caused all of my own problems, and it's up to me to maintain a healthy lifestyle," Greg said.

After the meeting, we went outside and lit up. It was breezy, and not too hot. There were clouds in the sky, and I thought the view from there might make a good painting. Julie seemed to be in a good mood, as I was; we always felt better after sharing something sincere. I was learning more and more about Julie by the things she was saying in the meetings, which she was afraid to share with me directly. It was interesting that we could talk to a large group about things we couldn't say to each other.

"I'm going home," I said to Julie. "Do you want to come with me or get a ride with Greg?"

"I'll come with you," she said. "What's the matter?"

"Nothing. I don't feel like hanging out?" I said.

"We'll see you later," Julie said to Greg.

I didn't know what had come over me, but suddenly I didn't feel good.

"What's wrong?" Julie said in the car.

"I don't really know. I don't feel right. I'm still not perfectly comfortable with myself. It's weird. Right after the meeting I felt good. Then I didn't. There's something seriously wrong with me," I said.

"You're all right. You had a mood swing is all, or a small anxiety attack," she said.

"I'm not anxious, but I do feel depressed," I said.

"It'll pass. It always does," she said.

"When I was smoking pot, I never had mood swings," I said.

"Well, we're not going back to that. Gregory said these swings will go away after a while," she said.

"I guess you're right," I said.

We went to my house, and I got into bed. I was restless and didn't get any sleep. Julie cleaned up a bit and then watched TV. When I got up, I took a very hot shower, and then at the end, I turned the cold on. I felt invigorated and then made some coffee. Julie's eyes were closed on the couch, so I let her sleep. I thought about Jennifer; I had to make time to see her, but I didn't know how I would. I was beginning to get more and more attached to Julie and sometimes thought that I would marry her. I knew I wasn't in a good position to get married, but that didn't stop me from thinking about it. When Julie got up, she helped herself to a cup of coffee.

"How do you feel?" she asked me.

"Better. My mood is stable again. I should ask my doctor about my medication. I might not be on the right dose," I said.

"That's a good idea," she said. "My doctor prescribed this stuff that I don't even think works," she said.

"I think you'll have to go through some trial and error before you find the right one," I said.

"I hope I find something soon," she said. "Do you want something to eat?"

"I'm pretty hungry. What about you?" I said.

"I'll make a salad," she said.

I helped her make the salad, and we sat down to eat. She ate like a bird, and I devoured my food. I wanted a nice big hamburger and thought maybe we would get one later. I was happy sitting with her and enjoyed listening to some music. I felt like things were settling somewhat, but I couldn't get Jennifer out of my mind. My conversations with Jennifer seemed more interesting to me than with Julie, but Julie's talk revolved more on life experience, which I liked, too. I knew Jennifer would gain some of that experience as time went on, but was I willing to wait?

"I'm going to bring up the topic of honesty tonight," Julie said.

"Why?"

"I want to hear what everybody has to say. I rationalize a lot, and I think that's a form of lying to oneself. What do you think?" she said.

"We all justify things to ourselves. I think that's part of being human, but it depends on what extent one does it to," I said. "If you can justify using drugs or drinking, then you're in trouble."

"I wasn't thinking about that. I don't want to get high any more, but I definitely justify a lot of things to myself," she said.

"I justify being out of work, because I had a nervous breakdown, but I think I can really work again," I said.

"That's a legitimate reason. You have a lot of trouble handling stress, and teaching is very stressful," she said.

"Thanks for understanding. I give myself a hard time about that," I said.

"I justify feeling like a victim and feeling sorry for myself. I have to get over that," she said.

"You will, in time," I said.

After eating, I washed the dishes, and Julie wiped off the table. I put on some Stan Getz and wondered if Julie was in the mood for a little fooling around. We stretched out on the couch and snuggled. I kissed her on the back of the neck and started to rub her ass, slowly. She leaned her head back and kissed me. I rubbed my cock against her ass and put my hand on her breast.

"You don't have to lick me if you don't want to," she said.

"I want to," I said.

I pulled her pants off, as she took of her shirt and bra. Her panties were already wet. I put one finger in her pussy and licked her clit. I went slowly at first and then increased my speed. After a few minutes, she came and screamed: "Fuck me! Fuck me!"

I got on top of her and put my hard cock inside. She moaned, and I pushed it deep inside. As I was coming, I pulled out and came on her stomach.

"You didn't fake it, did you?" I said.

"No, it was great!" she said.

"Let's take a shower," I said.

We got in the shower, and she rubbed my back with soap. I knew she was still turned on, so I put two fingers inside her and massaged her clit with my thumb. After a couple of minutes, she came again.

"Stop now. It's too sensitive," she said.

I got out of the shower and dried off, while she washed herself some more. I put on a sweatshirt and jeans and made some coffee. I always smoked inside at my place, so I opened a couple of windows to air it out.

"Do you want to go out for dinner?" I said to Julie.

"Sure, if you can afford it."

"I've got a little money," I said.

We went to a small restaurant in Fayetteville and had a good meal. We didn't talk much during dinner. The food was good, and I was thinking how nice it would be to have a glass of wine. Then I thought about the nightmare of my drinking and smoking days and quickly put the wine out of my mind.

"Sometimes I'm afraid to tell you how I feel," she said.

"Why?" I said.

"I don't know. I'm worried you'll think I'm weird or something," she said.

"I'm weird, too, so don't worry about it," I said.

"My thoughts are crazy sometimes, too," she said.

"Everybody's thoughts are crazy," I said.

Driving home, I noticed that Julie seemed content for a change. When she felt good, I felt a lot better. Since we were both on emotional rollercoasters, we rarely felt great. At my place, we took a quick nap and got ready for the evening meeting. We got there early, and Greg still hadn't shown up. Lisa pulled up right after us.

"Hey, what's going on, guys?" Lisa said.

"Not much," I said. "We're feeling pretty good today."

"I had a fight with Greg," she said.

"Really? I didn't know he was the fighting type," I said.

"It was mostly me," she said. "I want him to go camping with me, but he won't go."

"Paul loves to camp," Julie said.

"No so much anymore," I said. "I like the comfort of my own bed."

"That's what Greg said!" Lisa exclaimed.

"You can't blame him for that," I said.

"He doesn't like to do anything but hang out and go to meetings," Lisa said.

"I'm like that, too," I said.

"But you're in early recovery," Lisa said.

"I expect to do more writing and painting as time goes along," I said.

"Sure you will," Julie said. "You might go back to teaching, too."

"I might," I said.

The meeting began, and Greg showed up a few minutes late. He had a big smile on his face, like he had hit the lottery or something. The topic was honesty, and Julie was happy about that. It was exactly what was on her mind. A lot of people expressed that it was important to not lie to yourself, no matter what you said to somebody else. I said that it was as important to not lie to other people. Gregory said that he had been perfectly dishonest when he was drinking, but that he was mostly honest now. Julie said that she didn't know if she was being honest with herself or not, and that it wasn't that simple. Lisa said that she was too afraid to be dishonest, that her conscience ate her alive when she was. We said other things as well, but that was the gist of it. I left the meeting in the middle to have a smoke. Afterwards, we went outside and sat on the picnic table.

"I'm curious," Greg said to Julie. "What is it that you lie to yourself about?"

"A lot of things, I think," she said. "Sometimes I tell myself I'm a good person. Sometimes I tell myself I'm bad. They can't both be true."

"You're a good person. I can help you out with that," Greg said.

"Thank you, but I lie to myself about other things, too. I don't always believe them, but I tell myself some bad things."

"You've got to change the tape in your head. Try to tell

yourself good things. You deserve to feel good," Greg said.

"Why is it that I tell myself bad things?" she said.

"You feel ashamed and guilty. You'll get over it eventually, but the sooner the better," he said.

"How do I get over my guilt?" Julie said.

"Keep telling yourself that you were a sick person, and that now you're getting better, and that you'll make up for the bad things you've done," Greg said. "Pray a lot and make amends when you're ready."

"I hope you're right," she said. "I hate feeling the way I do."

I hadn't realized that Julie felt so badly about herself. She had a good way of disguising it. I could tell that she was troubled from time to time, but now it sounded like she was tortured. It was difficult to tell how she really felt, especially since she was reluctant to discuss it with me. I didn't feel that bad, and I was noticing that slowly but surely, I was feeling a little better every day.

Chapter 12

On the way home, I felt a strong urge to reach out to Julie. I didn't usually find it difficult to say what was on my mind, but at that moment, I didn't quite know what to say.

"Are you all right?" I said.

"I was thinking about what Greg said," Julie answered.

"I didn't know you felt so much guilt and shame," I said.

"I've told you that before," she said, "about my daughter and everything that went on with my ex."

"I guess so, but I didn't realize it was so intense," I said.

"I can't stop thinking about it," she said.

"Like Greg said, you have to start thinking about other things," I said. "Think about the beauty of recovery and about me."

"I do think a lot about you," she said. "That's why you're so important to me."

"You're important to me, too," I said.

"You don't feel any guilt or shame, do you?" she said.

"Not really. I have a good way of forgetting the past and moving on. I look forward to next year and the years after," I said.

"It must be nice. I'm almost haunted by my past," she said.

"Can't you look forward?" I said.

"It doesn't look that bright to me," she said.

When we got home, I brewed a pot of half coffee, half decaf. Julie took a hot bath, and I relaxed in front of the television. I watched a movie for a while, then went into the bedroom to see how Julie was doing.

"You know what I like most about you?" she said.

"What?"

"You're lighthearted," she said. "You don't take yourself too seriously."

"We're all clowns in this circus," I said.

"I take myself way too seriously," she said.

"Why don't you joke around a little more?" I said. "Or look at the beauty of the birds and the trees."

"I'm not as romantic as you are," she said.

"I think everybody else has the potential for being romantic, if they would only sensitize themselves to things," I said.

"You're making me a more sensitive person," she said.

"The world is simply too cold," I said.

She got out of the tub, and I dried her off. We watched TV for a while, then went to bed. She slept better than I did. It took me a couple of hours to fall asleep. I slept deeply though and dreamed, but I couldn't remember my dreams in the morning, no matter how hard I tried. We both got up at about seven, and Julie was kind enough to make the coffee.

"I feel better today," Julie said.

"A little bit better every day," I said.

"I have to go to the bank and the post office in the morning. Do you want to meet me after the meeting?" she said.

"Sure. I can run my errands afterwards," I said.

"We need to get some new curtains for the living room," she said. "The old ones are nasty."

"Why don't you simply move in here. You're here all the time anyway," I said.

"If you really want to, I will," she said.

"I want you to. We get along pretty well, and we're really

helping each other," I said.

"Oh, it's going to be so great, and I promise I'll pay my fair share," she said.

"I'm not worried about that," I said.

"I am. I've always supported myself, and I need to feel some dignity, so I'll contribute," she said.

"Okay, if that's the way you feel. The only thing I ask is that we not fight about money. I hate that," I said.

"I don't fight about much," she said.

She went to her apartment immediately and started packing. I told her I would help her move her furniture into a storage space and bring the rest of the stuff to my place. She was on a month-to-month lease, so she gave her landlord notice of her leaving. I was a bit apprehensive about her moving in, but I was willing to give it a try. We spent most of the day moving and went to the hall later in the afternoon. Greg and Lisa were already there.

"What's up, guys?" Greg said.

"We're living together now!" Julie said.

"That's great," Lisa said.

"What brought that on so suddenly?" Greg said.

"She's been over at my house all the time, so I figured I might as well ask her to move in," I said.

"I hope it works out," Lisa said.

The meeting started, but I lingered outside to finish my cigarette. I was feeling better about Julie moving in. As long as we didn't fight too much, I knew it would be a good experience. The topic that night was about trust, and I thought about how my mother had stopped trusting me.

Julie said: "Everybody in my family lost trust in me. I stole from my parents, my husband, and once even left my daughter by herself at home for a few hours, while I went out and drugged.

Now I'm beginning to rebuild the trust, but I know it'll take a long time."

When it was my turn to speak, I hesitated for a moment, then said: "I have trouble trusting myself still. I don't know if I'm going to be able to stay sober. I don't know if I can carry on a relationship, and I don't know if I'll be able to go back to work. I'm getting better slowly, and I know I only have to stay clean today, and as long as I stay close to my sober friends and keep going to meetings, I have a shot at this. Thanks for letting me share."

Greg talked a while about building up trust with his family and friends and said he was able to finally get married, which was the highlight of his life. Lisa said she was on a strong footing now, too, and how grateful she was for the meetings. Afterwards, we went outside, as usual, and smoked. I was getting annoyed with all my smoking and became resolved to quitting soon.

"I feel better," I said.

"Me too," Lisa said.

"Me three," Julie said.

Greg laughed and lit up a big cigar.

"Where'd you get that?" Lisa said.

"From Larry," Greg said.

"I'm glad you didn't buy it. We hardly have enough money to get by," Lisa said.

"I'm going to work again soon," Julie said. "I'm doing school and work."

"Easy does it," Greg said.

"Why don't you go to school and forget work for right now," I said. "You can't concentrate on school if you're working at the same time."

"You don't mind supporting me for a while?" Julie said.

"No, I told you. I'll pay the bills. You go to school," I said.

"All right with me," she said.

It was getting dark later and later as we approached the summer, and the evenings were beautiful. We decided to go home after talking to Greg and Lisa for half an hour, and I was pretty tired. I was thinking that I would start a regimen of swimming in the afternoon. I had been a good athlete in high school and was now badly out of shape, though I wasn't heavy. Slowly but surely, I was beginning to establish a routine, which I had lacked for a long time. I had been clean and sober for most of my twenties and now was trying to get back to the feelings I had had then. I had had a lot of success in the early part of my life, and I was hungry again for more success. I thought about Jennifer for a second but knew that that was over.

"Do you want to take a bath with me?" Julie said.

"No thanks. I'm going to bed early," I said.

"Do you think we're making a mistake living together so early in our relationship?" she said.

"No. I think it'll be fine," I said.

"I'll make breakfast in the morning," she said.

"We can sleep in a little," I said.

I was getting used to sleeping with Julie, and I think I was sleeping better than when I had been alone. There was something emotionally satisfying about being with a partner that I had lacked before. Julie was very loving and always thought about me, which I was not used to. I went to bed and had trouble getting to sleep, until Julie slipped into bed with me. I dreamed wonderful dreams that night, but I couldn't remember the specific content in the morning. I slept pretty well, and we stayed in bed until nine.

"I have a question for you that I've had on my mind for a

long time," Julie said, as we drank our coffee.

"Go ahead," I said.

"How can an atheist be spiritual?" she said.

"Same way everybody else is, except we don't pray to God," I said. "Most of us atheists are very careful thinkers, who have strong morals. We try to be loving, sensitive, and care about others. I don't have to tell you that a lot of believers are hypocrites."

"Sometimes I feel like a hypocrite," she said.

"That's not your problem," I said.

"What is my problem?" she said.

"You have a few, but mostly because you're in early sobriety. A lot of your problems you create yourself, and most of them will be straightened out as you stay clean and sober," I said.

"I don't have a lot of patience," she said. "I want most of my psychological problems solved now."

"You have to work through them. Why don't we meditate again today?" I said.

"How do I work through this? I can't seem to make any progress," she said.

"You will take one problem at a time. Try to be relaxed, and not fret so much," I said. "You have to slow your mind down. It races too much."

"The meetings help, but an hour afterwards, my mind starts racing again."

"We have to get you on the right medication, a mood stabilizer like lithium or Depakote," I said.

"Which do you take?" she said.

"Depakote, and it really helps," I said.

"Okay, I'll go back to the doctor this week," she said.

We decided to meditate and put a candle between us. We

stared at the candle and repeated a word in our minds. Half an hour later we stopped and smiled at each other.

"That works better than medication," she said.

"For a while," I said.

I took a shower first. Then Julie did. We were being pretty lazy that morning. We had already missed the first meeting. We went shopping for a few things for the apartment, and I bought about a dozen different candles. We had a sandwich at a local deli, and the day seemed perfect. When we got back, there was a message on the machine. It was Jennifer.

"I miss you. I'm sorry for everything, and I want to see you soon," she said.

Julie, of course, was furious. I explained to her that I had ended it with Jennifer, and that there was no need to discuss it further. Julie finally calmed down, but we didn't talk for an hour. We put up our new curtains in silence, and it looked lighter in the apartment.

"Let's meditate again, maybe for twenty minutes or so. I could use it," I said.

"Good idea."

We meditated for twenty minutes and felt a lot better afterwards. I thought about Jennifer a little while I meditated, but I tried to keep her out of my mind. We sat in front of the television, and our relationship normalized again.

"Why don't you give Greg a call?" Julie said.

"All right," I said.

I dialed Greg's number, and Lisa answered.

"Hi, sweetheart, how are you doing?" I said.

"I'm fine. What's up?"

"I thought I'd give Greg a call, but if you want to talk to Julie first, you're welcome," I said.

"Sure. Let me talk to Julie," she said.

"Hi. How are you?" Julie said.

"Fine, I guess."

"Paul's old girlfriend left a message on our machine," Julie said. "I wasn't too thrilled about that. Paul reassures me there's nothing to worry about."

They talked for a while. Then Julie handed me the phone.

"Hi," I said.

"How are you, brother?" Greg said.

"I was having a good day until Jennifer left a message on my machine that Julie heard," I said.

"That's not good," he said. "You'd better end it with Jennifer once and for all."

"You're right," I said.

"What else is going on?" he said.

"For the most part, we're getting along very well. She forgave me about Jennifer, and I told her it was over. I think she's getting better about letting things go," I said.

"It's going to take a lot of time," he said.

"I know," I said. I'll see you at the meeting."

"See you," he said.

I wasn't used to having a woman around all the time, but I was determined to get used to it. I liked my freedom and was afraid to have children. I knew Julie wanted at least one other child, and it scared me. I liked children but was afraid of the commitment. After I hung up the phone, I sat on the couch with Julie and listened to music. Jazz made me feel better. It relaxed me and made my thoughts slow down.

"Do you want to make love later?" I asked her.

"We'll see," she said, laughing.

"Does that mean yes?"

"Probably," she said.

"Do you feel like cooking tonight, or should we order pizza?" I said.

"How about I make us a nice vegetable soup?" she said.

"Sounds good, and we'll have some bread with it," I said. "Will that get you in the mood?"

"You're so horny all the time. What is it with you guys?" she said.

"Be glad I'm healthy," I said. "One day I might not be able to get it up."

"You'll be able to get it up until you're ninety," she said, laughing.

After dinner, we went to the meeting. Lisa and Greg were outside, sitting on the picnic table. It was a cool night, but the stars were out, and it felt great to be sober. I reflected for a second about how lonely I had been for so long, even in a relationship, and how grateful I was now to be in love.

"Hey, what's up?" I said.

"Chillin'," Greg said.

"I'm going to bring up a topic," I said.

"What's that?" he said.

"Gratitude," I said.

"Things have changed, I see," he said.

"Yeah, we're doing better," Julie said.

"I'm very happy to hear that you're finally going in the right direction," he said.

The meeting began, and it wasn't too crowded. Everybody was drinking coffee late in the evening, and I was, too. Julie whispered into my ear that the coffee would keep me up at night, but I didn't care. I was in a good mood. Like most people in recovery, I drank a lot of coffee, but it didn't seem to bother me too much. I raised the topic for the meeting and really enjoyed hearing what everybody had to say about gratitude. When it came to my turn, I hesitated for a moment, then said: "I am so grateful, mostly for the people that have helped me, including Julie here, and my family. I couldn't have done it without the people at these meetings, in particular Greg and Lisa. I have the best friends I have ever had, and I have a feeling of hope, which is invaluable. Thanks."

Julie's turn was next.

"The most beautiful thing about recovery is how I feel. I didn't have feelings before. I numbed myself and was afraid to feel pain. Now I can feel the pain and know that I can get through it. I also have feelings of love, hope, and joy, which are remarkable for me. I can't express my gratitude to you all. Thanks."

She was almost in tears saying that, and I felt very close to her at that moment. Greg and Lisa spoke, and they, too, were filled with gratitude. After the meeting, we went out and smoked, but Lisa was trying to quit, so she was chewing gum.

"That was a good meeting!" Julie said.

"They're magical, aren't they?" Greg said.

"Why do we feel so much better afterwards?" Julie said.

"Talking helps reduce one's problems," Greg said. "There's something about the power of communicating our difficulties that simply puts them into perspective, like therapy."

"I can't believe how good I feel," she said.

"I feel good, too," I said. "Let's go home."

"Okay," Julie said.

It was getting late, and I wanted to make love to her before I got too tired. I asked her to drive my car. I wanted to relax. It was a beautiful night, and I truly felt great. I thought if it didn't get better than this, it was fine with me. I also knew that my mood wouldn't remain elevated, but I was still getting better. When we got home, I put on some coffee and turned on the music. She knew what I was thinking even before I said anything.

"So, you think you're going to get some, huh?" she said.

"How do you feel?" I said.

"Great, and I'm in the mood," she said.

We went into the bedroom, and I pushed her on the bed. I lay next to her and began kissing her passionately.

"I love you," I said.

"I love you, too," she said.

We made love, and I was overwhelmed with emotion and passion.

"Will you marry me?" I said.

"Why don't we wait a while," she said.

"That's all right with me," I said.

Five months later, we were engaged.

CPSIA information can be obtained
at www.ICGtesting.com
Printed in the USA
JSHW030948170223
37766JS00002B/68